# The Zochtil

*Almek Manning Book 1*

By J.A. Dalley

This is a work of J.A. Dalley
http://www.almekmanning.com
Copyright © 2012 by James Andrew Dalley

Cover Art by Graphicz X Designs
"Call of the Sirens" © 2011 by Craig Dalley, used by permission of the author

ISBN: 978-0-9858049-0-9
PRINTED IN THE UNITED STATES
First Printing: August 2012

*To Robert A. Heinlein*
*Who for over eleven years has inspired me with his*
*works of science fiction.*

*Special Thanks to Isaac Stephens*
*Who helped me create the Draconians and has read*
*every draft I've given him and provided excellent*
*feedback.*

# Chapter 1
## Aboard the UES *Mayflower*

I was sitting at my desk on the first faster-than-light ship ever built. Well, maybe not the first ever built, but the UES *Explorer* and the USS *Independence* had both exploded when they tried to go FTL. On the UES *Explorer,* the captain had been in communication with Earth when he pushed his ship from point nine-niner to one c.

"Transferring to FTL," he had said.

"Roger," NAV COM had replied. "Good luck!"

Then in one brilliant flash, picked up by thousands of satellites and telescopes aimed at the *Explorer,* she had exploded. It was almost as if the ship had hit a wall. Parts of the ship were flattened, while other parts just couldn't be accounted for. Whether they were vaporized or went FTL was a mystery that scientists still hadn't figured out.

The worst part was not that the ships had exploded but that each one had been packed full of colonists. Entire civilian families had died, and yet the UES *Mayflower* was packed with more civilian families ready to colonize another world.

I was one of those colonists and wasn't scared. Sure, I was only ten, but my father, the captain of the UES *Mayflower,* wasn't scared. A man named Randy Kelven was the reason that we all believed the *Mayflower* would survive.

The *Mayflower* was accelerating toward the Kelven threshold, the speed at which, theoretically, the Kelven Drive would be able to slingshot us faster than light.

We were just passing Jupiter, and our speed was at about point eight c. My dad's chief astrogator, Andrus, said it would be another couple days before we reached point nine-niner. Even though I was on a mission that would rewrite history, I still had homework. In addition to the useful stuff, like math, I also had to do literature, even though there can be no possible point in reading a book written before the internal combustion engine was invented. Seriously, who cares if some idiot tried to joust with a windmill?

"Okay," I said, shoving my homework across the desk to my tutor, Jared Belnap, a petty officer in the United Earth Navy. "I'm done with it, you can check it now, Belnap."

"Will do, twerp," Belnap said, getting up. I could tell that Petty Officer Belnap enjoyed math tutoring about as much as I did, because he always called me twerp.

I fidgeted as he went over my work, marking all the things I had done wrong. After about ten minutes, he handed it back to me.

"Rework those problems," he said. Then he looked at his watch, "Have them done by class time tomorrow. I have to stand watch now."

I wanted to be a starship captain, like my father, but I didn't relish all the work I would have to do to get there. I much preferred playing computer games or learning about the ship's systems. I wanted to learn astrogation, but Astrogator Andrus said I would have to wait until I had mastered differential equations and fractal geometry. But I was itching to do things, not just learn.

***

A couple days later, the crew of the *Mayflower* was bursting with excitement. The passengers, on the other hand, were nervously pacing the corridors, reading their scriptures or praying that the Kelven Drive would work, while the crew was busily preparing to switch to the Kelven Drive. Even my mom was a little nervous, and she told me I didn't have to do schoolwork. So, I headed down to the wardroom, looking for my friends in the Marine Corps.

The UES *Mayflower* included a detachment of twenty marines in case we survive faster-than-light travel, in case we reach Centauri B, and in case we find anything dangerous there. The marines weren't very happy about being aboard. They thought the three months they'd spent on the *Mayflower* had been a complete waste of time. They spent most of their time in the mess hall, either eating or playing RISK. RISK wasn't my favorite game, but it was fun to join them occasionally.

The marines weren't at all nervous. They just sat around their usual table, with a couple games of RISK running at the same time. Their captain had the best version. It had a map of the solar system, and your troops (or marines, as they always called them) had to travel across the system to attack other worlds. Since it allowed landings on Jupiter and Saturn, it didn't achieve the height of realism, but it was still fun.

I sat down next to the captain and watched him take his turn.

"Hey, boot," he said. He had called me boot since the first day he met me back earth-side. He seemed to think that I wanted to be a marine, even though I had told him my plans were to join the Navy.

"Hi, Captain," I said. "You winning?"

"Yes, sir. Today I've got Luna, Ganymede, Titan, and Jupiter. And my troops are en route to Earth."

I watched them play for a while, until the captain won, then I joined in a new game. We played a couple hours before the captain won again. I swear the captain had the dice rigged to always roll in his favor, but I couldn't figure out how he could have managed that. I used the same attack and defense dice, and they still always rolled in his favor. After the captain had won the game, I got up and went to the bridge to visit my father and mother.

After visiting the bridge, I was actually bored enough to get back to doing my homework. There just wasn't a whole lot you could do in space if you were unemployed.

\*\*\*

I was awakened the next day by the sound of the boatswain calling out, "All personnel to your duty stations. All off-duty personnel strap down. We will be testing the Kelven Drive in ten minutes."

Ten minutes wouldn't give me much time. I ran out into the hall, and went straight to the bridge. I reached the bridge with four minutes to spare. My father glanced at me.

"Welcome, Almek," he said. "You can have Advisor Firmin's chair. He was feeling sick this morning and won't be reporting for duty."

I nodded and sat down silently. I knew the gravity of the situation.

"Astrogator," my father called out. "What's our speed?"

"Three minutes from the Kelven threshold, sir," he said.

"Jessica, put me on the all-hands circuit."

My mother nodded and pressed a couple buttons, "You're on, Captain."

"All hands, this is the captain speaking. We will be testing the Kelven drive shortly. Everyone must fulfill their duties perfectly. Good luck, and see you on the other side of light speed." My father nodded to my mother, and she cut off the circuit.

"Captain," Lieutenant Kelven called out over the speakers.

"Yes, Randy?"

"She's primed and ready, sir," Kelven said.

"You sure, Randy?"

"As sure as I ever will be, Captain. There is nothing left to do but test her out, except perhaps praying that I didn't drop a decimal point."

"Don't worry," Father said. "You've already got everyone on the ship praying for that."

"One minute remaining, sir," Andrus called out.

"Good luck, Kelven," my father said.

"And good luck to you, sir," Randy replied.

I heard a click from the astrogation panel, and I turned to look at Andrus.

"Thirty-seconds … Twenty … ten … five … four … three … two," Andrus called out, as he read his display.

"Cut power to the main drive," Father said. "Bring the Kelven drive on line."

The main drive died, and I went weightless for a couple seconds. Then suddenly colors blurred together, everything around me went dark, and I couldn't hear a thing. I thought that I must have died. The Kelven Drive hadn't worked, and we would be just one more horror story for space-happy young kids like I had been. Then everything came back. I could see color, I could hear. We were alive!

I looked up at my father.

"Kelven, what just happened?" he asked with a detectable edge in his voice.

"We just surpassed light speed, sir."

"Andrus, what's our speed?" my father asked.

"We are going at one point two c. We've done it, sir!"

"Run a full diagnostic on the sensors. Make sure they are operating properly. Then we'll celebrate."

There was a long pause. "All the sensors are working, sir," a senior chief petty officer called out from his duty post.

My father smiled. "Then it is done. We have passed light speed. Jessica," Father turned to Mother, excitement beginning to show on his face, "I want a direct line with NAV COM."

"I'm on it, Captain," she replied.

My father turned back to Andrus, "How long until we reach Centauri B, Andrus?"

"We will reach our destination in ten days if we follow the planned speed profile."

"Good, follow the plan, and consult with Kelven. If he says you need to make any changes, follow his orders exactly."

"Yes, sir," Andrus replied.

"I've got NAV COM, sir," my mother called out.

"Captain," I heard NAV COM say. "What happened? You aren't showing up on any of our scans."

"We've done it," my father said. "We're traveling at one point two c."

I heard a huge roar from NAV COM and assumed that everyone there was celebrating our success. "Congratulations, sir!"

Father turned to his commander. "Commander O'Brien, how would you like to take command of the first FTL starship?"

"I'd love to, sir," Commander O'Brien replied.

Commander O'Brien was a reservist in the Navy, and, once we reached Centauri B, he would be the governor of the planet. My father didn't like him, because he was just a politician and not a real naval officer, but my father couldn't be on the bridge all the time.

"On the bridge, this is Captain Andrew Manning, Commander O'Brien has the conn," my father called.

"This is Commander O'Brien," O'Brien echoed. "I have the conn."

My father waved at my mother and me, and we both got into the lift tube heading down to our quarters.

"What do you think of this, Almek?" my father asked.

"I thought I was dead," I said. "When all the lights went out, and I couldn't hear. I thought that Lieutenant Kelven had failed."

My father sighed, "I did, too, son."

"Well," my mother said to me. "You just witnessed the single most important event in the history of transportation."

"That you did, son," my father agreed.

\*\*\*

We had just sat down to dinner with Andrus, Kelven, and the other department heads, when we were interrupted by news from the bridge.

"Captain," O'Brien said. "Relative velocity is reading zero, sir. The Kelven Drive is no longer operational!"

"What?!" Kelven shouted. "I go away from that darned girl for one second, and she starts acting up."

"What happened?" my father demanded.

"I don't know, Captain. Just get up here on the double." O'Brien swore. "Hurry! Over twenty ships appeared directly ahead of us."

My father sprinted for the nearest ladder, with my mother, Andrus, and the department heads on his tail. Kelven took off for engineering, and I ran for the nearest lift.

I stepped out of the lift to see O'Brien stalking off the bridge with the master-at-arms. Then I looked up at the main viewer. I saw dozens of ships, all of which resembled dragons from a medieval fantasy. Suddenly, an image of a humanoid dragon appeared on the screen.

"I am the commanding officer of the Draconian blockade force. Humans are to stay within the confines of this solar system! Report this back the chair of United Earth, before we destroy you for firing on us."

Huh? Had Commander O'Brien fired on the dragon creatures? After a brief pause, the dragon ships all began to open their maws, and lasers started pounding the ship's hull.

My father jumped into action. "Jessica, order the call to abandon ship, and raise NAV COM. Then get out of here!"

She complied, grabbed me, and we ran off the bridge for the escape pods.

"NAV COM," my father was saying. "I have twenty-six alien ships firing on me. I am transmitting all the records of the ship to …"

I was off the bridge. I was split from my mom in the crowd heading for the pods, but the marine captain found me.

"Boot!" he shouted.

"Captain!" I cried. "You found me."

"Come on, we've got to blow this place."

He picked me up, and carried me like a football to an escape pod.

"You," the captain said, pointing at his sergeant. "Find the boot's mom, and tell her he's safe."

"Wilco, Captain," the sergeant replied.

Then the captain closed the pod's hatch, and we launched. I looked at the Petty Officer who was piloting the pod, and then I glanced down at his screen. I saw a mass of yellow dots, which represented the escape pods. I looked through the view port and saw that the dragon ships were firing on the pods. I saw many of them vaporize. Then something very strange happened. I saw a massive blue spiral appear ahead of us.

"Sir," the petty officer said, looking at the captain. "I've lost control of the pod. We're being pulled into the spiral!"

"Can't you turn us around?" he demanded.

"No, sir. The controls just aren't responding, sir. I can't get any yaw or pitch."

"Well, then, let's face death like marines."

"But, I ain't a marine, sir," the petty officer said.

"That's obvious," the captain retorted.

I grabbed the captain's arm, and clung tightly to it.

"That's all right, boot," he said. "You are a true marine."

I smiled. It made me glad to know that the captain thought well of me. I had always sought his respect.

Then we entered the spiral. Seconds later we exited, and right there in front of us was the most beautiful sight I had ever seen. It was Earth! All blue, green, and cloudy, just waiting for us to return home.

# Part 1
# London Proper

# Chapter 2

## On the Bank of the River Thames

I was sitting on the bank of the River Thames, though the Thames is no longer like I've heard it once was. It had once been a major tourist attraction of one of the greatest–if not the greatest–city in Europe. However, the Thames no longer shows the same splendor, and no tourist would dare venture near it today. The Thames was once a beautiful blue, but is now green, brown, grey, and sometimes even blood red. The Thames runs with the blood of those who call London home.

London, like the River Thames, is not what it used to be. The once great city that had been the heart of the United Earth Government is now a bombed-out wreck. Skyscrapers, once towering, now lay strewn across multiple city blocks. Shopping center parking lots are still full of cars, and the cars are full of shrapnel or have been ripped in two by small cluster bombs. Houses lay in ruins, with roofs caved in. Driveways have been destroyed, windows broken, and the city is deserted.

Mostly deserted, I should say. London has turned into the dumping ground of the new United Monarchy of Europe. London Proper is where all the criminals in the western part of the UME are dropped off. It is much cheaper than paying for real prisons, or even killing the criminals. Thus, London has turned into a desolate place where only the worst live, and it has been renamed The London Proper Detention Facility.

Yet, here I was on the bank of the River Thames in the middle of London Proper. I wasn't a criminal but an orphan. I was an orphan who had refused government protection, so I had been thrust onto the streets of London Proper. I wasn't actually an orphan, except in the legal sense of the word. My father had died on the *Mayflower*. He went down with his ship, as every captain should. My mother and I made it back to earth, thanks to the blue wormhole, which has not yet been explained.

My mother resigned her commission after the cease-fire. She took my father's death hard, and she eventually turned to drinking. When she was drunk, she turned on me and blamed me for my father's death. She went mad. Two years after the cease-fire the Child Rights Police came and took her away. I haven't seen her since. She probably ended up here in London Proper, too, but I don't think she could have survived.

I was not alone. I was sitting next to a beautiful and battle-hardened young lady. She was tall, about five foot eleven, with short brown hair and gorgeous brown eyes. Long hair wasn't practical on the streets–it was just too likely to get in the way during combat. Her name was Annabeth Gauge. She was my girlfriend and my most trusted confidant.

I knew that I should have been with my squad. We had just won a battle, but we had lost many, many good men and women. However, my squad knew I needed to take this time with Annabeth and let the atrocities of the battle flow out of me. We had just beaten our greatest enemies: two squads who had allied to try to defeat my squad. Those squads were commanded by Duke and Drake. Drake had been my archenemy, but now he and his squads were all gone. We had killed every last man and woman. My vibroblade was still stained with blood. I had spent the past several minutes attempting to wash the blade clean and had finally given up. The battle had been too long and the River Thames too dirty. Nevertheless, we had won.

My squad and I no longer had anything to fear in London Proper. We had beaten all who tried to fight us, and we were now the most powerful squad and the rulers of London Proper, and I was the squad leader. I turned from my thoughts to face Annabeth.

"Annabeth," I began. "We've done it. We've finally done it."

"Yes, we have, Almek. We have, but it isn't enough, is it?"

After a long pause, during which I turned once more to face the River Thames, I said, "No. It isn't."

"You need to go into space, don't you? You need to serve in the Fleet."

She was referring to the Solar Fleet, the space navy of the Presidential Council. The world had been racked by a massive civil war, which had torn apart United Earth. The UME, on the one side, consisted of Europe, Russia, the Middle East, and most of Africa, while the PC, on the other side, consisted of Australia, the USA, Canada, South America, China, and Japan. After having been so badly treated by the UME, I felt that my future lay with the PC and the Solar Fleet–not with the UME.

"Yes, I need to go to space," I said, my gaze shifting upward to the moon, which was faintly glowing in the sunset. I wanted to space! I wanted to serve in the Solar Fleet, as I'm sure my father would if he were alive today.

I often wondered what my father would think of me being stuck here in London Proper, the squad leader of a gang of teens and young adults, ravaging a city for food, killing for food, killing to stay alive, acting more like a savage than a man, and certainly not like an officer in the navy.

"Annabeth," I said, turning to face her again. "What would … will the squad think?"

She sighed heavily. "The squad knows you, and most of our squad wants to space, too. But after a battle like this, I don't know if they're ready."

"But I am … I am. I need to get out of here, Annabeth. This isn't my home … I don't belong here. Why did we have to kill them all? Why wouldn't they just surrender? Why did we have to kill them?"

Annabeth scooted closer to me and wrapped her arm around my shoulder, "Almek, you need to focus. Your squad needs you. You've been out here for an hour now. You've never been gone this long, and your squad will begin to wonder. We need to go back."

"Do I tell them?"

"Not now," she said. "We wait. Things are too tight right now. None of us wanted to kill them. Why they wouldn't surrender, I don't know, and none us are taking this victory well. We want to celebrate, but we killed so many. You don't have the luxury to mope. You've had your rest, and your squad needs you. You are Almek Manning, squad leader of the most powerful squad in London Proper."

"Is that something to be proud of?" I asked her, turning to look at the bloody vibroblade at my side.

"Whether it is or not, the rest of our squad is proud of it, so you have to act proud of it, too."

I sighed heavily, trying to force all the negative emotions out of me. "Aye, aye, ma'am. Let's go back to the squad."

Annabeth and I got up. I sheathed my vibroblade and slung my rifle over my shoulder. We hiked our usual route back to camp, but, when we were about a klick away, we were halted.

"Stop! Identify yourself!" a voice shouted, and it seemed to echo all around the empty streets. "I have you in my scope."

"Almek Manning," I said.

"You may pass." The shadowy form of a squad member appeared on the roof of a nearby shopping center. "You had us worried. You were gone an awful long time."

"I'm sorry, Kris," I said. "I had a lot to think about."

"I understand," she said. "I've enjoyed my time standing watch. I also needed the time to think and come to grips with my standing in the eyes of God."

"That too," I said. "I hope to see you 'round the fire later tonight, or do you have a longer watch?"

"I'm here until 1900, sir," she said. "Save some grub for me."

"I will. See you then."

Annabeth and I took a long and circular route to make it to the camp. I knew that Kris would have hopped on the radio and told everyone about my return from the Thames. However, it was still good to let those soldiers who were on watch see that their squad leader was ready to lead them again.

"Halt! Identify! I have you in my scope!" This voice I easily recognized–having heard it for over half a decade.

"Jen!" I shouted. "It's me, Almek Manning!"

Jenny was an interesting girl, to say the least. She stood six foot one, just a few inches taller than me, which she never let me forget. She had hazel eyes and short brown hair.

Jenny was the one who had saved me from death on the streets of London Proper for the first time. I had been wandering on the streets for only thirty-two hours when she found me. Having refused government indoctrination through the schooling system of the UME, I was deposited in London Proper. The Child Rights Police dropped me off on the streets, equipped with a one-way comm link to CRP headquarters in case I wanted to come back, though I later found out that the comm links were only good for twenty-four hours before the batteries ran out.

Jenny found me surrounded by a gang of Drake's teens. I watched her kill two of them that day. At thirteen, I had never seen death up close before. I'd seen my father's ship ravaged by lasers, and I knew that people had been killed on that ship, but I had never actually seen someone killed. Jenny had killed them coolly. She hadn't seemed to be fazed by what she had done. If only she'd killed Drake then, but Annabeth tells me not to dwell on the "ifs" …

Since that day, Jenny had helped me survive on the streets. She taught me the rules of the streets, taught me how to wield a vibroblade, how to jury-rig a laser charge, and many other skills. Jenny brought me to the squad she belonged to and vouched for me. She had been my mentor and guide for months, and we became best friends.

Now, after more than five years, I thought of Jenny as a sister. At some point, Jenny was no longer the one training me. I had learned all I could from her, and I begun training her. I couldn't explain this transition, nor do I have a clue when it happened. It was so gradual that neither of us really noticed it until long after the transition occurred. I also realized I was no longer happy living in that squad. I wanted my own squad. When I told Jenny, she gathered her weapons, and we left. She didn't ask any questions, we just left. We set up camp on the border of London Proper and started picking up kids who were brought in by the CRP. We also picked up a handful of UME deserters deposited in chains at the edge of London Proper and left to die. Jenny became a part of me over the past half decade. I didn't know what I would do without her.

That thought brought me back to my present needs, and I said, "Jenny, you get yourself off watch. I want you at the officers' meeting."

Jenny laughed. "Are you kidding me, Almek? I'm not on watch! Kris radioed down here and told us you were on your way. I've only been up here for the past five minutes. I just wanted to get your head in my scope. Let you know that your officers have your back."

"Thanks, Jen. Come on down. I can smell some grub cookin'. Who's the chef tonight?"

"Unfortunately, it isn't me. I was too tired, so Kai volunteered."

"Kai ain't half bad," I said.

"No, he's not."

"Well, see you indoors."

Annabeth and I entered the small office building where we'd taken up residence. Miraculously, the office building had not been bombed. Half a decade of disrepair had left its mark, but the building was good enough for me and my squad. As soon as I walked through the doorway, I was greeted by my dog. Sapphire had been my first friend in London Proper, even before I met Jenny. I'd run into Saph only moments after being dropped. She was a beautiful Golden Labrador, with a very strange design on her forehead, a deep blue five-pointed star. She kept me alive until

Jenny found me, and since then she had been a stalwart companion, having saved my life multiple times.

I knelt down and petted her. "How you doin', girl?"

She just glanced up at me, and nuzzled my chin.

"It's good to know that you're doing good," I said. Then I stood up, so that I could take in the whole camp.

I saw the cooking fire burning brightly in the corner, and my eyes lingered over the scorch marks on the floor from where we normally lit our bonfires during the winter. I glanced over the men and women cleaning their vibroblades or field stripping their rifles and handguns. I ignored all of them, and made a beeline for the men and women who were being tended by Kate, my squad's healer.

She was one of the deserters Jenny and I had picked up. She had been a corpsman on a UME ship when she went AWOL. She was caught after only two days and deposited in London Proper, without so much as a court martial.

Before the battle, my squad had been fifty-one strong and the combination of Duke's and Drake's squads had totaled forty-seven men. We'd killed them all, but I had lost fifteen, with ten additional injured. Our casualty total was almost fifty percent. It was a high price to pay.

I walked over to the wounded. Kate's head was bent over one of the injured soldiers. She was one of the few people who refused to cut her hair short, and her long blond hair covered half of her face. She was gently wrapping a fresh bandage around the man's arm, her hands moving carefully so she wouldn't cause any more pain.

"How are you holding up?" I asked her.

She didn't reply until she tied off the bandage, then she glanced up and flicked her hair out of her eyes. I saw her deep blue eyes were filled with the pain of the suffering around her.

"I think we're going to lose Samantha."

"Is there anything I can do?"

"No, Almek. Just don't get us into any more battles."

My heart wrenched, because I knew that I was about to do just that.

"I … I can't make any promises."

"I know," she said, sighing heavily.

I knelt down by each injured soldier and spoke words of praise and gratitude to each of them. They needed to know that we all appreciated the sacrifice that they had made, that it was worth it and, most importantly, that their squad would never forget the price they had paid.

When all of them were healed and in fighting condition again, we would total thirty-six soldiers. Would that be enough to escape London Proper and the UME? I didn't know, but I would soon find out. I shuddered inside, wondering how many more I would lose, and if I could really ask them to do this for me.

I headed over to the cooking fire where Kai was at work. Kai was one of the old navy hands like me. Both his mother and father had served in the United Earth Space Navy. His dad was a naval aviator, and his mother an engineer. He had also been dropped off by the CRP when he had refused to go through indoctrination. He wasn't even a UME citizen; he had just been unlucky and ended up in UME territory when the war started. I knew that Kai was just as anxious to space as I was. We spent many a sleepless night gazing at the stars and discussing our hoped-for future in the navy. I was sure that he would be more than happy to escape with me.

I sat down next to him and waited for my cadre of officers to gather around. Jenny came down the stairs, still toting her rifle. She walked over to our armory, deposited it, and then joined us. Spencer came over next. He'd been sitting next to one of the injured soldiers, a man from his platoon. I looked around, searching for his brother Collin, and soon found him. He was sitting in the armory, playing with some empty charges for the rifles. He was trying to recharge them. I watched his long fingers nimbly working on the charges. It was funny to see his tall, lanky form intensely hunched over those small charges.

Collin was probably the most important member of my squad. He was my squad's techie. He rigged all of our radios and could come up with amazing ways of recharging the clips for handguns and rifles. Collin was one of my original squad members. We picked him up one month after I became squad leader and, without him, my squad wouldn't have survived much longer. He gave us the technological advantage that most squads didn't have. Most squads had a handful of guns, along with a few half-used charges, but every member of my squad had a gun that had charges to spare. Collin's parents had been anti-UME revolutionaries. Their group had revolted, and the revolt was crushed. The UME marines had killed every adult and then dumped their kids in London Proper.

My gaze circled the camp, looking for the last member of the cadre, Marian. Marian was the oldest person in my squad. She was twenty-two, and she was the toughest fighter in our squad. She was deadly with or without a weapon. Marian kept mostly to herself. I didn't have a clue where she came from or how she had ended up in London Proper.

Kai finished cooking and called Kate over. She and her medics quickly dished out ten bowls of soup and took them to the wounded. Then Kai called the soldiers. They lined up to get their food. Once the others had dished out their food, it was the officers' turn. In most squads, the leaders ate first, but that wasn't good for morale. The squad needs to know that their officers will not eat unless their soldiers eat, and that soldiers will not go hungry unless the officers also go hungry. Not that my squad had to be afraid of going hungry. We controlled several acres of farmland that produced a variety of fruits, grains, and vegetables.

During the meal, we discussed rearranging personnel so that we would all have equal-sized platoons again. We talked about the new watch schedule, and other tasks. We were just talking shop, and it felt good.

After dinner, I called my squad together so that I could talk to all of them. I walked up to the stairs at the far end of the lobby, and I waited until everyone was silent.

"Men and women," I said to those in the room and, via radio, to those on watch. "You have all earned your keep today, many times over. Today we may rest knowing that we have nothing to fear. We have won! We have proved we are the best of the best! I congratulate you!

"However, I do not want to see any of you slacking for even a moment while on watch. If you start to fall asleep on watch, or to be less alert, you will be disgracing the memories and the lives of your comrades, your brothers and sisters in arms who died today to give us this liberty, this freedom, this peace of mind. Our worries may be smaller now, but do not forget your squad mates who died today. Remember that we are the Manning Squad! Thank you for fighting hard today! Thank you for fighting well!"

The room broke out into cheers and applause. Life was good in London Proper.

# Chapter 3
## Preparation

Three weeks later, my squad was ready for battle, though I had suffered the loss of one more soldier. Samantha had indeed died, as Kate predicted. She died when a broken rib punctured her lung. There was nothing that Kate could do with the technology we had at camp. My squad was down to thirty-five, and we were about to attempt a raid on a UME naval base.

Kai and I were far outside the borders of London Proper. We had traveled over the electric fence through the use of a contraption that Collin had created. He had tried to explain how it worked, but I finally gave up and was satisfied with the fact that it *would* work. Kai and I were on a hill overlooking the UME Naval Base, located thirty kilometers upstream along the Thames from the border of London Proper.

"What do you think?" I asked, passing the binoculars to him.

"It will take more than thirty-five people. Only a handful would be able to escape, and we'd lose a lot."

"What about Kathy's squad?" I asked him. Kathy was the leader of the first squad I had joined, and our squads often worked together. "We could ask her squad to join with ours and have them lure the marines out of the base. Then those of us who want to escape could sneak in, steal a ship, and bug out."

"How do we lure enough marines out?"

"Okay, so how about this, my squad attacks the east gate," I said. "We kill the guards just as Kathy's squad blows a ton of C4 by the main gate. The part of my squad that doesn't want to leave falls back to this hill to provide a diversion. Kathy's squad falls back to the ditch by the main gate. Meanwhile, those of us who are leaving make use of Collin's expertise to breach the east gate, so we can steal the ship and get out."

"This is a naval base," Kai said. "They've got everything from jeeps, to helos, to jet fighters. Those who are left behind *will* be killed."

"Once we steal a ship, they're going to focus most of their firepower on the stolen ship."

"It would only take one beat up helo to kill those of us who don't go."

"Those who stay behind should be able to keep the navy at bay with our RPGs. Then once they get back to London Proper, they'd be able to disappear."

"*If* they get back."

"Well," I said. "We've got another week to plan this out, then we'll be going. Every man and woman on this mission will be a volunteer. After we plan the op, I'll present it to the squad. And they can either join us or stay back."

I took the binoculars from Kai, and we spent another two hours drawing maps of the base. After that we packed up and headed back to London Proper. We climbed over the fence where Kris was standing watch, waiting for us to return.

"Welcome back, squad leader," she said. "You had us worried. You'd been gone for almost eight hours."

"It's a long walk," I said. "And I told you not to worry about me unless I wasn't back by nightfall."

"Well," Kris said. "Jenny is a little overprotective, but she's your XO."

I took Kris' radio and walked out of earshot.

"Almek calling Jenny."

"This is Jenny," her voice responded after a millisecond. "You made it back safely?"

"Yes, Jen," I said. "I want a meeting with Kathy. Tonight preferably."

"Can do," she said. "I'll send Kris … no she's with you … I'll send McCloud then."

"Sounds good. I just want to see her at camp tonight."

"She'll be there. See you shortly."

\*\*\*

We trekked back to camp, and I called my officers together. Once they all arrived, Kai and I laid out the maps we had drawn. We explained a couple of the ideas we had about how to get in.

"I don't like it," Kate said, settling deeper in her chair after Kai and I had stopped talking.

"Why not?" I asked. "I want to know about any flaws in the plan."

"You're asking your soldiers to sacrifice themselves for you."

"They'll be volunteers," I said.

She swore at me. "You know that everyone of them would die for you if you asked them. Not a one of them would hesitate for a nanosecond. You're going to be using your men. They trust you, and you are going to be breaking that trust."

"You may be right," I said. "But the decision still lies in their hands. They have the choice."

"I still don't like it. These soldiers have earned their keep here in London Proper. They deserve a rest," Kate said.

"So," Jenny said. "You're saying that you want to stay here?"

"Yes," Kate said. "I served in the mil, and I didn't like it. I don't believe that the Solar Fleet would be much different. I've found my purpose here as a healer, not a corpsman."

I nodded my head in thought. "I understand. I don't expect you to come with us then."

"I'm with Kate on this one," Spencer said. "This isn't right."

"I, of course, stand with Almek," Annabeth said.

"I just want to get in the cockpit of a space fighter," Kai said.

"I'm with Almek," Jenny said.

"So am I," Collin said.

"Ruff!" Sapphire added.

"Well," I said. "I hope you change your minds before we head out, but, if not, you have the freedom to choose."

"Sir," George McCloud said, approaching the table where we were sitting.

"What is it, George?" I asked.

"Kathy's waiting outside, sir."

"Escort her up," I said.

"Will do, sir."

My officers and I stood up and delivered a sharp salute. She returned the gesture with a casual salute and a smile.

"Your squad acts too much like a military organization," she said as she sat down.

"I like to run a taut ship," I said.

"Ship? You're not in the Navy or the Fleet. You're land locked on the streets of London Proper."

"That's what I wanted to talk to you about."

Kathy cocked her head to one side and raised an eyebrow.

"I want to get out of London Proper." I let that remark hang in the air for a long time, and then Kathy laughed.

"How do you expect to get over the electric fence?" she asked.

"I already have."

Kathy's jaw dropped. "How did you manage that?"

"You'd have to talk to Collin to get the details," I said. "But I've crossed the fence, and I've already scouted out the UME Naval Base."

"The UME Naval Base?"

"I intend to hijack a hovercraft and use it to get to America."

Kathy leaned back in her chair and started laughing. "You expect to hijack a UME hovercraft? Then what? Just cruise back to America? You'll be chased the whole way, until they put you out of your misery and blow you out of the water."

"That's not your concern," I said. "I just want your help in getting into the base."

"Just? You just want me to risk the lives of my squad members in your crazy and vain escape plan? Not in my lifetime, mister." Kathy stood up.

"Kathy," I said. "I know it's a lot to ask, but once I'm out of here, your squad will be the top dog out here. You'll own London Proper. You'll get all the land that my squad owns, all the farms we've created. You can have it all, along with the members of my squad who don't want to come with me."

I saw a glint in Kathy's eyes. My squad had a lot of good real estate and the best farmland in London Proper. Kathy put her hands on the table and leaned forward.

"What's your plan?"

I laid out the plan, then I sat back in my chair while Kathy studied the maps.

"It's no good," she said. "I'm not risking my neck or my men on this scheme." Before I could protest she raised a hand. "However, I do have an idea. Collin, can you rig some of your guns to fire on auto or when they detect movement?"

"Yeah," Collin nodded. "I'll need some time, but I could do it."

"Okay," Kathy continued. "So at night we go in and set up the guns. Then we lay the C4. When we're all set up. Your squad members who want to leave can make a go at it. We blow the C4, and you sneak in. I'll take a few of our elites to provide live fire. Once you guys are in, we'll bug out, and let the rigged guns do the rest of it. We could also plant C4 in other places and blow it at strategic times to provide a little more confusion."

I thought about it for three or four minutes without saying a word, then Kai finally broke the silence.

"I like it," he said.

I put all four legs of my chair back on the ground. "I do, too. Let's get ready. Collin, I need you to prepare the guns and get our equipment ready for this op."

"Will do, sir," he said and left the room.

"Kathy, can I have you announce this to your squad?"

"I will. Have you announced it to your squad?"

"No. I'll do that tonight."

"Okay then. I'll meet with you tomorrow to work out the details."

"Sounds good."

Kathy stood up. Everyone else at the table stood and saluted her. She just smiled and waved at us with a small shake of her head. As she left, I glanced around at the faces of my officers. Most of them showed determination, all except Kai. His face was lit with pure joy at the thought of leaving the wasteland called London Proper.

***

That night I addressed my squad.

"Men and women, I have a proposition. Most of you know that some of your officers are not happy living here in London Proper. We have always dreamed of bigger things, but, while we had the distraction of Duke and Drake to deal with, we had to postpone those dreams for the good of the squad. But, now, we are the top dogs. We are the best of the best, and so we have time to dream again. With the help of Kai and Kathy, I've developed a plan to allow us to escape from London Proper. I need to know who among you would be willing to risk your lives to escape."

Kai stepped forward. "We need two groups of people. I need to know who would be willing to facilitate our escape by playing sniper against UME navy personnel and marines and who wants to break out of London Proper. Those willing to facilitate the escape, step over there," he said motioning to the outer doors. "And those who wish to escape step over here with me."

As Kate had predicted, most of the squad joined the group who wanted to facilitate the escape. A handful, three to be exact, joined the group who wanted to escape.

"I'm delighted to see so many volunteer," I said. "However, I won't need that many of you. I'll probably pick ten of you to accompany those of us who wish to leave. I'll have more information for you shortly. Until then, just pretend that nothing is going on. For those of you wondering who will be in command of this squad once my officers and I are gone, let me clear that up. You will be merged with Kathy's squad, and she will care for and protect you. With her as your leader, you will be unassailable as the most powerful squad ever to walk the streets of London Proper."

With that, I stepped down from the stairs, and signaled for the three who wanted to leave to follow me to the officers' wardroom. When we got there, Kate was already waiting for me. I nodded at her and turned to the others.

"Kris Taggart, Ryan Tulev, and Alan Shelton, I'd like to know why you wish to leave London Proper."

There was a brief period of silence before Kris responded. "I want to enlist in the Solar Fleet."

I nodded, "Enlistment, huh? You'll make a great NCO, Kris."

"Thank you, sir," she nodded.

"I want to go to college and live a real life," Ryan said.

"Same for me," Alan agreed.

"Those are good enough reasons in my book," I said. "I just wanted to know. You are dismissed, except for Taggart."

Ryan and Alan saluted, then left. Kris stayed behind at attention, but with a question in her eyes.

"Kris," I said. "Surely more people want to leave London Proper for the same reasons as Ryan and Alan. Why didn't more volunteer to go?"

"May I answer this one?" Kate said, standing up.

"Sure."

"Because, they all know that only a small handful will be able to successfully escape. If you have too many people trying to escape, you won't succeed. Everyone understands that, so no one else volunteered. However, every single one of them expects you to come back for them, at some point. Every day, they are going to wake up and look towards America or look up towards the moon wondering when you will come for them. Most of your men worship you. They had nothing when they came here, and you gave them something, everything. Every one you leave behind will expect you to rescue them, and, if you truly care for them, you'll come back as soon as possible."

"Thank you for speaking bluntly, Kate," I said. I turned to Kris. "I hope that you'll serve under me again in the Solar Fleet."

"I do too, sir, but let's focus on getting to America before we start plotting too heavily about what we'll do once we get there."

"Kris," I shook my head, lost for words. "You're awesome."

"Thank you, sir," she said.

"Dismissed."

# Chapter 4

## Escape on the River Thames

"Okay," Collin said, standing over piles of equipment. "First," he explained, as he put on a dark helmet, "this is our protection from flash-bangs." He showed how the headphones worked as noise canceling receivers. He had also equipped each helmet with high quality sunglasses to reduce the brightness of flash-bangs.

"Second," he continued, "your weapons. I haven't changed anything on these, just extended their charges and added silencers.

"Third," he showed us the C4 detonators and explained how to use them.

"Fourth," he showed us how to set up the automatic guns.

"Fifth," he gave us the tools he'd made to allow us to climb the fence.

"That's it from me," he said and then stepped back, allowing me to take the floor.

"We all know the stakes, so let's do it!" I said, punching the air.

We all put on our packs and headed out. We quickly climbed the fence and headed out on the long trek to the naval base.

\*\*\*

With the help of a cloudy moonless night, we had set up everything without being noticed. I stood in front of my squad members who had volunteered to help us escape.

"Good luck," I said. "I *will* come back for all of you as soon as I can."

"Thank you, sir," one of them said.

I walked down the line of men and women and shook everyone's hand. Then I reached Kathy.

"Thanks, Kathy," I said. "I couldn't have done this without you."

"No prob," she said. She gave me a hug, "Let's get her done."

"Yes, let's."

Then we went our separate ways. My much smaller squad found the spot that Kai and I had scoped out earlier. Kai and I both attached sniper scopes to our rifles. These had been hard to come by. We had won them from a gang a couple years ago, and they had proved to be very useful.

There were four guards at the east gate. If we could kill them without raising the alarm, our escape would be much easier. Kai and I divided up the guards and scoped in on our targets. I got one of them in the cross-hairs of my scope. I slowed the beating of my heart, exhaled, waited for my heart to beat, then pulled the trigger. I saw my man crumple, and I scoped in on the next. I had to move fast to get him before he saw his downed mates. I heard the soft discharge of Kai's rifle. I exhaled, waited, and fired. The second guard went down. I scoped in on Kai's second man, but before I could get him in my cross hairs I saw him fall and heard Kai's rifle discharge.

Kai and I stood up from our kneeling positions and congratulated each other.

"Let's move!" I said.

Jenny, Kai, Spencer, Kate, Marian, Collin, Alan, Ryan, Kris, Saph and I snuck up to the gate, arriving there in just a couple minutes. Collin put his pack down and pulled out our squad's only computer. He hooked it up to the keypad on the gate and pulled up a program he had crafted. Five minutes later, the gate slid open, and we were in.

"Okay," Collin said. "I've got their cameras running a loop right now, but I don't know how long it will keep their computers fooled."

"So far, so good," I said. "We haven't sounded the alarm yet. Annabeth, you're our navigator. Where do we go?"

"This way," Annabeth said. "I hope."

"Kathy," I spoke into my comm link. "We haven't been intercepted yet. We are in the base. Await further instruction."

"Will do," Kathy said. "Good luck."

We stuck to the shadows of the buildings as much as possible; we didn't want to alert anyone by being careless. We had traveled about a kilometer when sirens went off throughout the base. We needed to get to the docks quickly!

"Kathy! Now!" I said.

"Roger."

A couple seconds later, we all heard the sound of explosions. We looked towards the main gate and saw a huge cloud of rubble.

"Let's move faster!" I told my squad, and we ran in a dead sprint towards the docks.

It wasn't long before we heard the sound of a jeep coming up the road behind us.

"Do we take them or take cover?" Kate asked.

"We take them," I said. "Annabeth, Jenny, go to the other side of the road. When the jeep gets near, Jenny, Marian, and I will jump in front and start firing. Then Annabeth and Kai will hit them from the sides, while Ryan and Alan hit them from behind."

"Sounds good," Jenny said. "Let's do it!"

The rest of us waited, while Ryan and Alan ran along the ditch at the side of the road to get into position. Then Jenny, Marian, and I jumped in front of the jeep, shooting at the machine gunner standing on alert in the back. Kai and Annabeth joined from the sides, and Ryan and Alan blasted them from behind. The marines never had a chance.

Then came something I'd been dreading: the unmistakable sound of helos. They were going after Kathy and the others.

"Faster!" I shouted. "Collin! You're driving! Everyone pile in!"

Now that we had the jeep, we were able to travel faster. When we reached the docks five minutes later, we found about thirty marines guarding the three hovercrafts. Two of them were in dry docks, and the only one on the water was the one farthest from us.

"We're going for the ship that's afloat," I said.

I quickly positioned my men, and we hit the marines. I had flipped my rifle to automatic. The thirty guards found themselves under the automatic fire of nine rifles. Within thirty-seconds half of the marines were down, but those left had began fighting back. The dock was full of crates, blocks of metal, and other materials. The marines threw a handful of flash-bangs at us, which would have quickly ended the operation if not for Collin's handiwork with our helmets. The marines were a little cocky and jumped out to take us prisoners after they had thrown the grenades.

Spencer raised enough from behind his crate to empty a charge into them, but he took a blast to the head.

"Kate?" I called over the comm.

"He's dead," she said.

I didn't respond. We had all known the risks were very real. Then one of the marines threw a frag and took out Alan and Ryan. I swore.

"Cover me!" I shouted.

I couldn't allow them to continue throwing frags. The others laid down heavy covering fire, and I advanced a couple of crates farther. Then I lobbed a small package of C4. I heard the marines gasp in shock, then I hit the detonator. In the confusion of the explosion, the rest of my squad advanced and eliminated the last of the marines. We ran for the ship.

We made it as far as the ramp before the reinforcements arrived: ten jeeps full of marines. Kate, Saph and I were still on the shore, and we were pinned down by the jeeps with their automatic weapons.

"Collin, how long will it take you to bring this ship to life?"

"Not long."

Jenny and Kai were providing covering fire from the deck of the hovercraft, but the enemy fire was too thick for either of us to make it.

"Kate, you go first," I said. "I'll throw C4 as a diversion, then give you covering fire."

Kate looked at me with determination in her eyes. "No," she said.

"What?"

She took a deep breath, "This isn't my dream. It never was. This is your dream. You go. I'll cover you."

I was about to protest, but she stopped me.

"It's the only way for you guys to make it out of this alive." Her blue eyes were filled with pain. "Just remember to come back for the others."

I hesitated.

"Give it to *me*!" she shouted.

I gave it to her, "Kate, I *will* come back."

"Good! On three. One … Two …" she tossed the C4. "Three!"

The C4 exploded, and she jumped up from her cover. I ran with Sapphire at my heels. I just made it to the quarterdeck when the engines roared to life.

The ship shuddered to life, and we started to move. I turned to look for Sapphire. I glanced around, but Jenny grabbed me and pulled me behind cover.

"Saph was right behind me," I said.

She pointed, and I saw her limp body on the ramp.

I glanced back at the dock and saw Kate's body slumped over a crate. Her body was riddled with laser blasts, and her long blonde hair was stained with blood. Her body was lifeless. She was gone. She'd made fun of the squad for being willing to die to help me and escape, yet, all along, that was what she had intended to do. She had come along to make certain that our escape would succeed. I gave her one last salute as the hovercraft moved away from dock and out into the Thames.

Jenny led me to the bridge to talk with Collin.

"How does she look?" I asked him.

"Pretty good," he said. "It appears she has plenty of fuel, and all systems seem operable. Annabeth reported from the Combat Information Center, and we are fully stocked with weaponry. So, all in all, I'm happy."

"Good," I nodded. "Kai, Jenny. I want the two of you to get into the AA turrets and prepare for helo boarding parties."

"Yes, sir," they responded in unison.

I found a seat on the bridge and tried to make sense of all the controls before touching anything.

"We have helos inbound," Annabeth reported from CIC.

"Kai, Jenny, how copy?"

"Good copy," both of them confirmed.

I looked out the windows of the bridge into the moonless night. The high clouds would work to our advantage, because the running lights on the helos would really stand out. I heard the AA guns start firing. Kai and Jenny took down three helos, and I saw the rest of the helos pull back.

"They don't want to damage the ship," I told everyone over the comm.

"That's lucky," Kai said. "It wouldn't have taken much to destroy one of these AA guns."

"The real trouble is going to be once we get to the mouth of the Thames," Annabeth said. "They can't fit the biggest ships in the Thames, but once we leave the Thames, we can expect to be surrounded."

"Thanks for the encouragement," Collin said.

"Any time."

When we reached the mouth of the Thames, we found that Annabeth was right.

"I'm picking up a lot of ships," Annabeth reported. "It looks like about fifty."

"Say again?" I asked.

"I repeat–*fifty*. They seem to be in two groups, though."

I walked out onto the deck and looked through my binoculars. The sun was just barely beginning to light the horizon, and I could see a little.

"Some of those are Presidential Council ships, specifically US ships!" I shouted. "Collin full power! Head for the US ships!"

We had traveled half the distance to the US ships when we received a transmission from the flagship.

"This is the USS *Lincoln*. If you continue to charge at us, we will consider it an act of war, and the treaty will be broken."

I punched the comm button. "This is HMS *Defiant*. This ship is being captained by Almek Manning, son of Captain Andrew Manning. I am seeking asylum in the United States."

"This is the commanding officer of the *Lincoln*. Say again," a different and stronger voice said.

I repeated and waited for a reply.

"We are sending a boarding party. If you fire on them, you will be destroyed."

"Roger."

"Slow your ship to one-third."

"Roger. Collin, slow to one-third."

I called for everyone to report to the deck. The helos arrived and deposited a team of SEALs.

"How many people are on board?" the lieutenant commanding the SEALs asked.

"Six," I responded.

The lieutenant stayed behind to guard us, as the rest went to search the ship.

"His story checks out," one of the SEALs said after they had finished the search. "There are only six people on the boat."

"Interesting," the lieutenant said. "Just where are you six from?"

"London Proper," I said.

He didn't appear fazed, but I figured that was just because he was a SEAL. He'd been trained.

"And how would a gang of teenagers steal a military hovercraft?"

I didn't see any harm in telling him, so I did. I told him everything from the details about our situation in London Proper, to the death of Saph and Kate. Once again, he retained his poker face. I still had no clue what he was thinking.

"Rumor has it that Almek Manning is in the employ of the UME." The lieutenant made the statement and watched for my reaction.

I wanted to emulate his cool demeanor, but I wasn't very good at it. I'm sure he could see the rage in my eyes. "Me? *I* would never work with or for the UME. I *hate* the UME. We should have colonies in multiple systems, not just Mars, Luna, Ganymede, and Titan. We should be spread throughout this part of the galaxy. But no, we have to stick to this one solar system because we're in the middle of a massive war with Europe. If I'm working for the UME, then you're an Army Ranger not a Navy SEAL."

The lieutenant smiled for the first time. "Nice analogy, kid. I wouldn't want to be mistaken for a Ranger. However, I can't just take your word that you are Almek Manning and not a spy. We will take you back to the *Lincoln* and turn you over to the commodore."

"Okay," I said. "Let's go."

Most of the SEALs escorted us onto a helo, and it took off for the Lincoln.

\*\*\*

"Petty Officer Richmond escorting the crew of the Defiant, who are requesting asylum," a sailor said as he snapped to attention in the commodore's stateroom.

"You are dismissed, petty officer," the commodore said, turning around.

I gasped in shock. The commodore was Chief Astrogator Michael Andrus from the *Mayflower*.

"Surely you recognize me, sir," I said.

"You look like him," the commodore said. "I would like to think that it is you, but I can't. What's your real name?"

"My name is Almek Manning. Son of Andrew Manning, formerly Captain in the United Earth Navy and commanding officer of the UES *Mayflower*."

"Drop the guise, kid," Andrus said.

I racked my memory for something that only I would know from the *Mayflower*. I came up with two things. "Sir, my math tutor onboard the *Mayflower* was Petty Officer Jared Belnap. I was also close friends with the marine captain on the *Mayflower*, Captain Nine. We often played RISK in the mess hall."

The Commodore looked startled. "That is something that not many know. Petty Officer Richmond," Andrus said, as he pressed a button on his watch. "Ask Captain Belnap to join me."

We waited in silence until Captain Belnap arrived. He smiled from ear to ear when he saw me. Belnap looked much the same, except for streaks of grey in his hair, and a scar that ran from his left ear beneath the collar of his uniform. "Twerp?"

"Petty officer, or, I guess, captain?"

"Wartime promotion, twerp."

"Captain Belnap, can you quiz this kid about what you two talked about onboard the *Mayflower* to confirm he is Almek?"

"Yes, sir," Belnap said.

He drilled me hard for about half an hour, then he looked back up at the commodore.

"Commodore," he said. "I would and will stake my commission on the fact that he is Almek Manning, son of Captain Manning."

"You may have to," the Commodore said thoughtfully. "Almek, just what is it that you intended to do?"

"Well," I began. "I'll put it simply. I want to join the Solar Fleet and get a commission."

"Good," Andrus said.

"Why, sir?" I replied, confused.

"Having known your father, I'm sure that you would make a brilliant officer, though it won't be easy."

"Why, sir?" I repeated.

"Because the President has ordered your arrest."

"What?" Belnap and I asked in unison.

"The President seems to believe that you and your friends are spies and wants to have you all taken into his custody for questioning."

"Sir," Belnap began. "Shouldn't that be Admiral Cestari's prerogative rather than the President's?"

"In standard practice, maybe," Commodore Andrus said. "But, by the book, this was an operation run by the United States, and, as such, the President has precedence even over Admiral Cestari."

"But you know what the President will do to him … them."

"I know, Captain," Andrus said, sighing heavily and sitting down. "Escort them to the brig, Captain."

"Sir?"

"That's an order, Captain!"

"Aye, sir."

Captain Belnap turned around and gestured for all of us to follow him.

"And, Captain," the Commodore said.

"Yes," he said, turning at the door to face Andrus.

"Prepare operation sixteen-twenty."

Captain Belnap smiled. "I was hoping you would issue that order. I will prepare for sixteen-twenty."

"Good. Dismissed."

# Chapter 5
## Explanations and Accusations

"Well," Jenny said, as we left the commodore's stateroom. "I want some explanations. Why are we being arrested?"

"No," Annabeth said. "I want to know what a US naval aircraft carrier is doing at the mouth of the Thames?"

"Well," Belnap sighed. "I'm an engineer, not a historian nor a politician, but I'll do my best to fill you in.

"To start off with," Belnap said. "The UME and the Council are currently in a very fragile cease fire. While some are struggling to get a peace treaty signed, hawkish politicians on both sides have been seeking any pretext for war."

"Which way are things leaning?" I asked.

"War, of course," Belnap said. "But not because of the politicians. The military is pressing the limits of the cease-fire terms. One day soon, someone is going to slip, and the cease-fire will be blasted to shreds. Something like your dumb stunt with the hovercraft would be all that would be needed to push us into all-out war."

"Anyway, why the aircraft carrier?" Annabeth asked.

"Sorry, young lady. We, that is to say, this fleet is here to protect a convoy of merchant ships headed to Holland."

"Holland?" Annabeth echoed.

"Yes, the goods they are transporting will be shipped from Holland via airplane to Switzerland, the only truly neutral country left in Europe."

"Why don't you just transport the goods via rocket from the US?" Kai asked.

"Because," Belnap said, "the UME doesn't want any rockets headed anywhere near their territory. But, the merchants weren't willing to let their ships go through unfriendly waters unprotected.

So the UME and the Council created another fragile agreement: the Swiss Merchant Treaty. Thus, the USS *Lincoln* has been stuck escorting merchants to and from Holland for the past six months or so. Not *my* preferred assignment."

"Merchant Convoy, huh?" Annabeth said. "That would make sense."

"Now for my questions?" I asked my girlfriend, not Captain Belnap.

"Sure," Annabeth said, smiling.

"Why does the President of the United States have it in for me, without even having met me?"

"Simple," Belnap said. "He has met you."

"Huh?" I responded.

Jenny had been examining the deck plates, but at Belnap's comment she jerked her head up and stared at him.

"Well, it's not exactly simple," the captain continued. "But he does know you. The President of the United States and Assistant Chairman of the Presidential Council is Commander Charles O'Brien."

"O'Brien? Like the XO of the *Mayflower*?" I asked. I had a hard time believing that anyone would elect him as President.

"Yeah," Belnap said, sighing heavily. "That O'Brien."

"Wait," I said, still confused. "So I know the guy, but why does he want me dead?"

"Well, you remember that Commander O'Brien was a reservist..."

"There's nothing wrong with reservists," Kai said hotly, since his mother had been a reservist before the war.

"No, no there isn't, but this particular reservist was a politician by profession."

"Of course," Kai said, flinching.

"Yeah," Belnap agreed. "And to make it even worse he got his degree in tax law."

"No wonder he's a bad egg," Kai said.

"Anyway, the bridge records from the *Mayflower*, which were sent to NAV COM, showed that O'Brien had initiated the hostilities with the Draconians. Those bridge records seriously injured O'Brien's political career."

"Huh?" Kris said. "I guess I'm dumb, but why's he President?"

"Yeah," Belnap said. "He had to really struggle, and some people, including the commodore and me, believe that he only got elected by unethical means. Anyway, he has blamed just about everyone serving on the *Mayflower*. That's how the commodore and I ended up here aboard the *Lincoln*. He has all of the *Mayflower* people marked. The only reason Andrus and I are still here is because we've made sure our careers have been squeaky clean, and Andrus is also good friends with Admiral Cestari and the Sky Marshal himself. If either of us disappeared, O'Brien would be caught.

"You, Almek, are just about the worst person in the world in his eyes. You are not only from the *Mayflower,* but you are the son of Andrew Manning, captain of the *Mayflower*, the guy who openly disgraced him in front of the whole world via the bridge records. Since it has been rumored that you work for the UME, he believes that he has sufficient cause to arrest you."

"Why did Commodore Andrus inform this O'Brien character that we were here?" Marian asked.

"He didn't. It was the SEAL lieutenant. He is a loyal supporter, I mean spy, for the President."

"Captain," I said. "You were talking about the prospect of war. Is the Solar Military, or more specifically, the Solar Fleet, ready for that move?"

"No," Belnap said simply. "The problem is Lieutenant Kelven."

"What?" I asked. "Kelven is dead."

"That's the problem, Almek. The genius is dead, and the K-Drive died with him. Not completely, of course, but the progress has been slow. The SFS *Sky*, our flagship, is the fastest ship in the Fleet, and it can barely pull four and a half K. Besides that, only about one-third of the Fleet's ships are FTL capable."

"If the battle is in our own solar system, why is FTL that big of a deal?" Annabeth asked.

"Well, let me show you." Belnap waved us into a room off of the hallway we were walking through. A couple of lower ranking officers were drinking coffee in a corner. The room must have been one of the officers' wardrooms. Belnap walked over to a large screen on one wall. He pressed a couple buttons, and a map of the solar system appeared.

"This shows the current locations of the planets." We were looking down on all nine planets, plus their moons. He pressed a couple more buttons, and the perspective switched to show the planets from a side view. "Now you can see the positions of the planets along with their angle from the sun. Another button was pushed and fleets appeared, some SF and some UME.

"Say the Sky Marshal orders this fleet here," he highlighted the fleet that was orbiting the moon, "to attack the UME fleet around Mars. Going sub-light, it would take almost a month to reach Mars. The UME fleet knows that the SF flotilla is on the way. The SF flotilla is one week out when the UME decides to send their fleet orbiting Titan to attack ours around Ganymede, a trip that, at the UME's best sub-light speed, would take three weeks. Our flotilla is larger, so we don't worry. Then as they reach our Ganymede flotilla, they send in three of their monarch-class FTL ships. That tips the balance. However, we have some of our best FTL ships currently engaged in a battle over Mars. If we send the FTL ships from Mars to Ganymede we'll lose the battle over Mars and possibly most of that flotilla. If we don't, we'll lose the Ganymede colony and that flotilla. Do you see the problem?"

"I guess so," Annabeth said. "The logistics are a bit more complicated than in London Proper."

"Yes," Belnap said. "And that would be a fairly simple scenario. A real battle would have a few more variables."

We walked out of the room in relative silence and then to the brig.

"I'm sorry to say this, but here are your quarters," Captain Belnap said, waving at a couple small cells. "Boys in this one, girls in that one. I hope you realize I hate doing this to you. I've got to ask you something, though. Which branch of the SM do each of you want to join?"

"The Fleet," Kai said.

"Same," Jenny said.

"The SF," I nodded.

"I'd enlist in the SF," Kris said.

"The SF, I guess," Annabeth said,

"SF R&D," Collin said.

"The Solar Marines," Marian said.

***

We sat in silence for an hour or so, before Kris sighed and stood up. "If I'd known you had enemies in such high places, Almek, I wouldn't have volunteered for this mission."

"I'm sorry, everybody. I'm so sorry," I sighed. "I had envisioned many hazards, but this is a twist I never would have predicted."

"I'm more ready to join the SF than ever," Kai said. "We've got to find a way out of here."

"Kai," I said. "If we want to join the SF, we can't break out of an SF brig."

Jenny finally spoke up. "What does sixteen-twenty mean?"

I had thought about that number a lot since Belnap had left us here. "I can only find one explanation for that number. Well, only one logical explanation for the number. I believe that sixteen-twenty is not just a string of numbers, but a date. A year, to be specific.

1620 was the year the original *Mayflower* landed at Plymouth in the colonial United States."

"So … ," Jenny prodded.

"I'm not sure, but it must have something to do with the *Mayflower* crew. I hope it is a way to get us out of this mess. That's why I'm not going to worry about it. If Commodore Andrus and his connections can't get us out of here, then there's no one else who can. I hate to say this, but we'll just have to wait."

"I was afraid you'd say that," Marian said.

"Personally," I said. "I'm exhausted, and I'm going to get some sleep."

The others nodded agreement. I grabbed a pillow, and lay on the floor. My dreams, as always happens after a battle, were filled with the friends I had lost. It seemed like I relived the scene with Kate a million times. The last time, I awoke with a jolt and found myself in a sweat. I sat up and clung tightly to the pillow.

"Annabeth!" I whispered.

"I'm up, Almek."

"I need the Thames."

"I figured you would. I wish we could sit on her bank and discuss our predicament, but we can't. We will probably never see her again."

"Annabeth," I muttered. "All I could dream was Kate sacrificing herself for me."

"She sacrificed herself for us, Almek," Annabeth whispered.

"But she didn't have to die. As the commanding officer, it was my duty to stay and allow the rest of you to escape."

"Almek, remember, no 'what ifs.' This is a 'what if.' I know you want to discuss this, but now isn't the time nor the place. If … when we get out of this mess, we can talk about it, but for now, we have other problems to cope with. You knew the risks of this mission, Kate knew the risks, we all knew the risks. Everyone accepted those risks, and now we have to live with the losses we suffered. Almek, we don't have time to mourn yet. We have to get ourselves unarrested before we have the luxury to mourn "

"You're right," I said. "But when this mess is over with, we must find a river, a creek, or a stream, and sit down and talk."

"Deal," Annabeth said. "Now, try to get back to sleep."

I lay down, but I didn't go back to sleep. I just waited to hear the footsteps I knew I would hear from the corridor outside the cell.

When they came, I sat up quickly, hoping to see Captain Belnap or even Commodore Andrus. Instead, I saw ten men, none of whom were in uniform. They all wore black suits and half of them were holding deadly-looking rifles.

"Up you come, all of you," one of the men with a laser rifle said. "We are here to escort you to see the President of the United States."

I nodded, stood up, and shook Kai and Collin to wake them. Jenny did the same with the girls. We were all standing at attention, as a petty officer came up from behind, and unlocked the doors to our cells.

The men were not gentle, but we had lived on the streets of London Proper, and their rough treatment didn't bother us in the slightest. I could tell Kai wanted to fight back, but one hard look stopped him from doing something stupid that would have gotten us all killed. The men escorted us to a black helo with no markings on it. They quickly searched us just to make sure we didn't have anything on us. We were roughly pushed into the back, and the five men with guns joined us. The hover drives on the helo quietly whirred to life, and it took off.

After a long flight, we touched down on the White House lawn, and we were roughly pushed out of the helicopter. They escorted us into the White House. After a few minutes of traversing hallways and riding elevators, we were in the Oval Office, and there he was. He looked much older than he had on the *Mayflower,* but that was to be expected of a president. President O'Brien just stared at me and my friends. After a long silence, O'Brien spoke.

"Almek Manning," he began. "By executive order, I have found you and your co-conspirators guilty of treason, espionage, and spying."

I was shocked. Certainly the President didn't have that kind of power. "How?" was all I managed to get out.

"The politics would confuse you, but I can, and I have. You will be executed by firing squad on the White House green in twenty minutes."

Collin went berserk. He turned, punched one of the gun carriers in the gut, and yanked the gun from his hand. He had just turned it around, and was pointing it at one of the other armed guards, when he was hit by four laser blasts straight to the chest. The gun dropped from his hands, and he hit the floor.

"Does anyone else want to die early? I just gave you twenty minutes to live. Apparently, that wasn't enough for this kid."

My blood boiled, and I wanted to strike. The guy Collin had punched was just getting up. He managed to look me in the eye and mouth sixteen-twenty. I calmed down. Commodore Andrus had a plan. We had to wait.

"No," I managed to say calmly, but with a hint of venom in my voice.

"Good," O'Brien said.

"We've stared death in the face before. We'll go down with pride. We'll face this like marines," Marian said defiantly.

I barely stopped myself from putting my head in my hands. That had been a really dumb thing for Marian to say.

"Marines," O'Brien said. "Just as I had concluded, the UME really is desperate to recruit marines who are so young."

The men, whom I assume were secret service agents, escorted us to a small holding cell in the basement of the White House.

Kai was about to say something, but I stopped him with a hand gesture, pointing up at a small camera mounted on the wall. He nodded, and we sat in silence. After a couple of minutes, the injured secret service man entered and handed us some papers.

"I have some standard legal documents I need you to thumb," he said. "They're for posterity's sake. We can simply thumb them after you're dead, but it's nicer to do it beforehand."

I glared at him, "You can do it afterward for all I care."

He mouthed sixteen-twenty again.

"Then again, I wouldn't want you or your fellow secret service men to handle me any more than is necessary to bury me."

I thumbed the documents, and so did the rest of my squad. I handed them back, and he nodded at me.

"I'll see you shortly."

He left, and our fate seemed a little less gloomy. I still wasn't sure what sixteen-twenty was, but I now had a stronger faith that it was actually something real, something that might save us.

Ten minutes...

Five minutes... Still nothing. My faith was wavering.

Three minutes...

At two minutes, the door slid open, and we were faced with the same ten secret service men, all of whom were armed. They jostled us and got us to our feet as roughly as possible. Then we were marched out to the White House green. I looked up, and I saw President O'Brien staring out through an Oval Office window. We lined up and stood ready to face our death like marines. The secret service men leveled their rifles at us.

Then we all heard the unmistakable sound of a sonic boom. A jet fighter had just rocketed over the White House. The secret service men were confused and turned to see what was happening. Then an A-100 Warthog appeared not far behind the fighter and leveled its gun at the secret service men, who were nicely lined up. The cannon flared, and the men went down. By then, the White House defenses had kicked into gear, and they blasted away at the Warthog. Warthogs were built to take a lot of damage, and it kept the defenses busy while a helo dropped out of a cloud. The helo landed in front us. I was glad my rescuers weren't using rotary-based helicopters, because no rotary helo could have pulled that maneuver. A small band of ten very familiar marines helped us in. We were airborne and moving steadily away when the helo extended wings. We were instructed to buckle up, and get ready for high g acceleration. The helo ... jet ... went supersonic and we were out of D.C. in a heartbeat. We touched down within half an hour and were transferred into a small commercial rocket. There I saw the rest of the marines who had served onboard the *Mayflower*.

"Andrus will be waiting for you up in the control room," the marine captain said. "It's good to see you again, boot. Too bad you decided to take the naval route like your old man. You would have made a good marine."

I laughed at him. "Maybe, but I'll try my hand at ship driving first."

# Chapter 6
## An Interesting Day

I noticed that the Captain was not in a marine uniform, nor did he have any insignia, either the Solar Marine Corps flag or the Council flag.

"Captain Nine," I said, addressing the marine. "Why aren't you in uniform?"

"Conduct unbecoming an officer," he sighed. "I made a stupid decision, but it didn't rate a discharge. I had a good JAG who defended me to the end, but he was up against the President's personal JAG, Lieutenant JG Silver. The commodore could have gotten me out of the mess, but it just wasn't worth it. The commodore promised he would get me back into the service if the opportunity arose."

"Is this the opportunity?" I asked him.

"I doubt it," Nine sighed. "The commodore said that it is more likely I'd get hanged than reinstated. When he mentioned your name, I called up my boys, and we came."

I glowed inside. Captain Nine was my kind of soldier. "Thank you," I said.

"Anytime, boot. Now, let's not keep the commodore waiting."

He waved everyone into the passenger rocket.

"The rest of you," Nine said, gesturing to the rest of my squad, "can buckle up down here. We'll call you up top if we need you. We'll depart as soon as Almek gets in the control room."

I got into the elevator with the captain on my tail. I got off at first class and started to walk down the aisle towards the stairway that would lead up to the control room. I had reached the door when I heard a shout from behind.

"Drop your weapons!"

I spun and dropped into a crouch, instinctively reaching for a vibroblade that no longer rested on my hip. I was stunned to see that I was facing a kid. Admittedly, he was probably about my age, but he didn't look battle-hardened like my squad members were. He seemed more afraid of the weapon he was holding than of the gun pointed at him.

"Kid," Nine said, as he gestured with his gun. "This is a joint operation, and it would sure be nice if you'd cooperate"

The stairwell door opened, and Andrus walked out.

"Midshipman Winters," Andrus said. "This is done under the orders of the Solar Fleet. I am a commodore, as you can see from my shoulder boards, and would appreciate your cooperation."

"How do you know my name?" the kid asked.

"Because," Andrus said, "I figured that you would be the most likely to cause trouble, having been a temporary third lieutenant in the Solar Marines."

As Andrus walked towards the kid, he passed by me. The kid was focused on Andrus and Captain Nine, and I was able to slip behind a couple of accelerations couches, allowing me to maneuver behind the kid.

"I don't believe you," the kid finally said. "This doesn't feel correct. An operation conducted by the SF or the SMC would be handled with proper protocol."

"There wasn't time," Andrus said. "I had five hours to assemble this op. I think it wasn't too bad, under the circumstances."

I was now behind the kid. Captain Nine saw me, and gave me a hand signal. I nodded and signaled back.

"I'll put my weapons down, kid," Nine said. He slowly crouched down, placed his rifle on the ground and took two handguns out of their holsters. I was sure he had more on him, but this might convince the kid.

"Okay," the kid, Midshipman Winters, said shakily. "Now kick them towards me."

Nine did, with the first two, but he kicked the third one past the kid and to my waiting hand. I snatched it up, grabbed the kid from behind, and pressed the gun into the kid's scalp.

"Drop your weapon please," I hissed in his ear.

"I don't think I should," he said.

"Drop the weapon!" I insisted.

He dropped it, but when it hit the ground, the charge cartridge was exposed.

I jumped away from the charge, dropping the kid, and ducked behind a couch. The exposed charge produced the effect of a flash bang. I had just enough time to get to cover and put my hands over my ears. I was up as soon as the sound died away. Winters had known the effect of the exposed charge. He now had Nine's rifle and was pointing it at the commodore.

"I don't think you want him to die," the kid said.

I knew we were working on a tight schedule. O'Brien would be on our tail quickly. If he wasn't already. We couldn't deal with this kid any more.

"I have killed before," I said coolly. "Have you?"

"Is that a threat?" the kid asked.

"No, it was a statement." I pulled the trigger and blasted the kid's arm, which made him drop the rifle. Captain Nine was on top of him in a nanosecond. The elevator door opened, revealing my squad and five marines.

"What happened?" a marine asked.

"Marian," I said. She had trained under Kate and was a fair hand at healing. "Help this kid. Andrus, shall we go to the control room?"

"Yes," he agreed. "You have really complicated things by shooting a fellow midshipman."

"Fellow midshipman?" I asked, confused.

"You are now a midshipman in the Solar Fleet. You haven't been sworn in yet, but you are now a midshipman and subject to the UCMJ. That is how I was legally able to rescue you."

"I am very lost," I said, shaking my head. "Let's just get out of here."

We climbed up to the control room. Andrus slid into the co-pilot's seat, and I took an observer seat meant for VIPs.

"This is the captain speaking," Belnap announced. "I am sorry for the delay and any inconvenience we may have caused you. I'm sure that Global Transport will reimburse you for the lost time upon arrival at the spaceport. All passengers prepare for gravitational alignment and boost."

Belnap's fingers flew across the controls, and I felt a slight tingle as I got a little lighter. Belnap had turned on the ship's gravitational field.

We went higher then I expected. A short jump to a spaceport shouldn't have required us to go higher than microgravity, but Belnap took us all the way up to a parking orbit. Once we were in orbit, Belnap turned to face the commodore. However, the commodore didn't look at Belnap. Instead, Andrus got up out of his seat and moved over to the communication panel. He quickly typed in a code and waited, leaning back in his chair. "Please Hold," flashed across the screen.

"Captain Belnap?" I asked.

"Yes?" he replied.

"Why do we have acceleration couches?"

He laughed. "This is a Global Transport ship. This ship was around when acceleration couches were still needed. It's just been retrofitted as a top of the line luxury cruiser. Only the rich ride this baby. It's supposed to represent the golden age of space travel. Hence the rocket shape, which is less than ideal for our current technology. It's what the public wants, so that is what Global Transport provides. The free market still thrives in Council territory."

I nodded. I was about to respond when the commodore stopped us with a wave of his hand. I glanced over at the screen he was staring at, which went from black to white, then switched to the face of a middle-aged man. The man wore the dress whites of the Solar Fleet. On his collar was the single golden sunburst of the Sky Marshal. The symbol of the Solar Fleet, with five stars arranged in a circle was visible on one shoulder board. The other shoulder board bore the symbol of the Solar Marine Corps, with five stars also arranged in a circle, thus showing that he was the only person in history to have taken his lumps in the Marine Corps and then transferred over to the Fleet and learned to conn a ship. This man was the first Sky Marshal: the man in charge of both the Fleet and the Corps. He was second only to the President of the Council, and much more powerful than even President O'Brien. If anyone could help me and my squad, it would be this man. Sky Marshal Bartholomew Kitt was inspecting us. We saluted sharply. The Sky Marshal smiled and waved for us to be seated.

"At ease," he said, and the three of us broke our salutes. "I assume you are Almek Manning?"

"Yes, sir," I responded.

"Your rescue mission was a success then?" he asked.

"Yes, sir," Andrus answered.

"Well," the Sky Marshal said. "Now, it's my turn to start a rescue op."

"What are we charged with?" Andrus asked.

"You are charged with article ninety-four in relation to mutiny and sedition, along with unlawful enlistment. Almek and his friends are charged with fraudulent enlistment, espionage, spying, and treason. Captain Belnap is also charged with mutiny and sedition. You are also being charged with about a hundred lesser charges, but there's no need to worry about them. I already have Commander Schmidt working on your case."

"I wonder what my dad would think of this," I muttered to myself. "I join the Fleet and get court martialed before I can even be sworn in"

"Your father would understand the circumstances," the Sky Marshal said. "He was a good man."

"You knew him?" I asked, surprised.

"Everyone above O-5 knew him. I was in the Corps back then, but I was a three-star general, so I talked with him. I even assigned the marines that served on the *Mayflower*. So, yes, I knew your father. Not well, but I knew him."

I couldn't believe the Sky Marshal had known my father. Then again, if my father had survived, he would probably be a four-star admiral, serving under the Sky Marshal.

The Sky Marshal got more serious. "I hope you get to stay in the Fleet. I wanted to have the top JAG on this case, but she's tied up with some treaty violation involving the UME, and I couldn't pull her off of that. However, she said Commander Schmidt is a rising star in the JAG Corps. Well," the Sky Marshal sighed heavily. "I'll see you at Ontario Spaceport. I'm sure we'll also be meeting O'Brien there, too. Good luck!"

His face faded from the screen. Captain Belnap flipped the intercom on.

"This is your captain. All hands, we have had a slight course change. We will be landing at Ontario Spaceport. Any passengers who wish, may disembark there. Afterwards, this flight will travel to its original destination. This rocket should reach Dallas Spaceport in two hours. We are sorry for the inconvenience. Any complaints may be directed to Global Transport. Thank you for your cooperation."

"Cooperation my tail!" I said. "There was a kid down in first class that just about ruined the whole op."

"Was that what the explosion was?" Belnap asked. "I'll have to hear the whole story over a beer at some point."

"Sounds like a plan. What's the ETA?" I asked.

"Twenty-five minutes."

"Request permission to leave, sir."

"Granted," Andrus said.

I headed out the hatch, and found Jenny and Kai sitting on either side of Richard Winters. I walked over to them.

"What's your name?" I asked out of politeness, even though I already knew his name.

"Midshipman Richard Winters," he said, glaring up at me.

I put my hand out, "I'm Midshipman Almek Manning. It's nice to meet you."

He was reluctant to shake my hand, "Are you really a midshipman?"

"Yeah," I said. "I just talked to the Sky Marshal. He confirmed my rank."

"I'm sorry for the trouble I caused earlier. I did make a mess of things, didn't I?"

"Yes, you did."

He put his uninjured hand out and we shook. Suddenly his face darkened, "What did you say your name was?"

"Almek Manning."

"As in Captain Andrew Manning of the UES *Mayflower*?"

"Yeah," I said. "He was my father."

"Wow!" the kid said. "You knew Andrew Manning."

"Yeah, just a little," I confirmed.

Then he changed the subject again. "Have you really killed before, or were you bluffing?"

I took a seat and told Richard about London Proper, and our escape.

"Wow, you've had an interesting day!" Richard said, after I finished my tale.

I burst into laughter. I had just told Richard that I'd almost died at least three times, four times if you included his attempted mutiny. And the best he could come up with was that we'd had an interesting day. I finally caught my breath while Jenny and Kai were still laughing, and Richard was staring at us.

"What did I say?" he asked, as the laughter faded.

"Richard," I said. "You just made the understatement of the year! An interesting day! You obviously have no idea just how interesting our day has been."

"Well," I continued. "Can we be friends and not enemies?"

Richard smiled. "Sounds good to me. I truly am sorry for trying to stop your operation. I served in the Marine Corps for almost a year, so I've got a bit of 'the few and the proud' in me."

"Hey," Jenny said. "You haven't told us your story yet."

"I'm eighteen. I graduated from an online high school when I was twelve, and I started at the Australian Aerospace University when I was thirteen. I graduated with a Master's when I was seventeen. Then I took an internship with the Solar Marine Corps Research and Development. I worked with Samuel Graves and helped him perfect his anti-grav field. I worked on the Kelven Project with SF R&D. Now I'm off to the Academy. I liked the Corps, but I want to be chief engineer of a starship, so that means the Fleet."

"Starship?" I asked skeptically. "Since the Draconians started their blockade, we haven't had any starships."

"That's why I wanted to join the Fleet," Richard explained. "We have to defeat the Draconians before we can have starships again. However," Richard said, lowering his voice conspiratorially. "I believe there are human starships exploring the stars right now."

"What? Who?" I asked incredulously.

"DSI."

"DSI?"

"Dalton Space Industries," Richard explained. "You know, the people that built Dalton Spaceways, Plymouth Station, and Island One?"

"No," I said. "This must be fairly recent."

"Well, DSI is a massive company. They started out as Dalton Spaceways, running a small commercial space station. They've just kept growing. They built Plymouth Colony Station, the first space colony. After that they expanded Dalton Spaceways. Once they had proven that a space station colony would work, they built Island One, which is bigger than Plymouth and Dalton Spaceways combined. The scientists in R&D believe that DSI is a couple years ahead of the SF in technology. Even more advanced than Australia! I believe that they have a way of getting past the blockade and exploring, but it's just a theory."

"Sounds like a conspiracy theory to me," said Kai, always the skeptic

We continued to chat about all sorts of things until we felt the full push of earth's gravity against us, and we heard the loudspeakers click on.

"This is your captain again," Belnap said. "All personnel who wish to disembark may do so. Those who wish to continue to Dallas remain seated. A new captain and pilot will be boarding shortly. Once again, thank you for your cooperation."

Captain Belnap and Commodore Andrus came out of the stairwell, and they waved for us to follow them down the ladder.

"Coming Richard?" I asked him.

"Can I come?"

"Well, there's going to be a court-martial, and I'm sure you'll be called as a witness so you might as well join us," I said.

"Well, I also need some more work on my arm, so I guess I'll come."

We all climbed down the ladder, then stepped out of the rocket onto a slideway. I looked up at the ship. In big golden letters on it's side was printed Global Transport XK-12. I smiled. At least in the fleet, our ships have real names.

# Part 2
# Dalton Spaceways

# Chapter 7
## The Military Courts Martial

Captain Nine took ten marines and hopped onto the slideway in front of us.

"I want to make sure that O'Brien isn't waiting to arrest us," he explained. "You guys wait and follow us in about two minutes. If you hear gun shots, stay put."

We waited two minutes, then got on the slideway. We were followed by the remaining marines from Nine's squad. We didn't hear any gunfire so we continued on our way. We found Captain Nine and his marines saluting the Sky Marshal. The Sky Marshal looked much more impressive in person, his dress whites practically sparkling in the brightly lit spaceport. The Sky Marshal wasn't alone, however. He was standing with four men beside him, who were all dressed in full battle gear.

"Fleet STARs," a marine whispered in awe behind me.

I made a mental note to ask him what a STAR was later. Then I turned to my left and I saw President O'Brien. He had over twenty secret service men dressed in standard black suits, all of them carrying automatics.

"Sky Marshal," Captain Nine was the first to speak. "What are your orders?"

"I order you and your men to drop your weapons and allow my men to arrest you."

"Will do," Captain Nine said. "Men, disarm. We are under arrest."

Captain Nine acted first and dropped his automatic and the two handguns I had seen earlier. Then he pulled out an additional handgun, a string of grenades, and two vibroblades.

I glanced over at Richard, who had made a choking noise. He looked a bit pale.

"He was still armed," he muttered.

"He's a marine," I replied.

The rest of Nine's men disarmed as their leader had done, and the STARs proceeded to handcuff the marines. One of the STARs led the marines away.

"Now to the real matter at hand," the Sky Marshal said.

"Yes," the President said. "I need to take the rest of them into custody."

"No, that you will not do," the Sky Marshal said. "As Sky Marshal I am relieving you of that duty, and I am taking them into my own custody."

"What about pre-trial confinement?" O'Brien asked.

"The court martial will be held on Dalton Spaceways. They will be in pretrial restriction to Dalton Spaceways."

"Exactly. They could escape," O'Brien said.

"No one can get through DSI security, and you know that."

"Wait," Andrus said. "What about the preliminary inquiry and the Article 32 hearing?"

O'Brien laughed. "The preliminary inquiry has already taken place, JAG Lieutenant Michelle Silver performed it. Her recommendation, based on the seriousness of the charges against you guys, was that we forego an Article 32 hearing and go straight to a general court martial."

Richard swore quietly beside me. "A general court martial."

"We will see you on Dalton Spaceways then," the Sky Marshal said.

"That you will," O'Brien accused him.

The remaining STARs gathered us up and led us away from O'Brien.

"And Bartholomew," O'Brien called after the Sky Marshal. "I'm not so scared of you that I'd back away from calling you out on Article 37."

The Sky Marshal ignored him and led us towards another ship. This one was very obviously a fleet ship, for it looked neither like a rocket nor a plane. It was clearly designed for space travel.

"Welcome to my private yacht," the Sky Marshal said, turning back to us at the hatch, "the SFS *Olympus*."

We started to board when the Sky Marshal put out a hand to stop Richard.

"How are you mixed up in this, Lieutenant Winters?"

"Sir? You know me?"

"You're the youngest marine third lieutenant. Of course I know you."

"I was involved in the rescue mission," he said. "It's a long story."

"And we have a long time before the trial," the Sky Marshal smiled. "We have a lot to talk about, but come on in."

"Where are Captain Nine and his marines being taken?" I asked.

"They are civilians," the Sky Marshal said. "And, as such, they are not subject to the Uniform Code of Military Justice. They will be tried by a Presidential Council court, in Australia, after your court martial is over."

The Sky Marshal led us through the corridors of his ship until we were in a small wardroom. He waved us to the table, and we all sat down.

"I've got a question, sir," Annabeth said shyly.

"Go ahead," the Sky Marshal smiled.

"What does Article 37 mean, sir?"

"Article 37 relates to unlawfully influencing the actions of a court. Effectively, O'Brien said he doesn't want me, as Sky Marshal, to support you and thereby prejudice a court."

Annabeth nodded her head slowly, clearly deep in thought.

"Okay, now for my question," he continued. "How is Third Lieutenant Richard Winters mixed up in this mess?"

Andrus, Richard, and I alternated in telling the story, and the Sky Marshal was smiling from ear to ear by the end of it.

"So, Richard tried to kill you, and now you're all old friends?"

I smiled too. "It appears that way, sir. It was just a big misunderstanding."

The Sky Marshal laughed. "A bit more than a misunderstanding, in my opinion, but to each his own. Andrus was right, though. Shooting another officer is going to make things a bit rougher for Commander Schmidt, but this whole court martial is such a mess, I'm not sure if it changes things much."

"Sir," Richard said. "I am no longer a third lieutenant."

"Really?" the Sky Marshal said. "It appears my intel is a little behind."

"Yes, sir. It is, sir," Richard said. "I am now a Midshipman in the Fleet, though not yet sworn in."

"Of course," the Sky Marshal said. "So the Corps wasn't for you?"

"No, sir," Richard said, explaining. "I want to be a chief engineer, sir."

"Yeah, that might be hard in the Corps. Based on the work you did for R&D, I imagine you'll have no problem becoming a chief engineer. Petty officer!" the Sky Marshal called out. A petty officer entered through the hatch. "Bring in drinks. The usual for me."

I ordered my favorite: root beer on ice, neither of which I'd had in a long time. The rest of my squad followed suit, all except for Richard, who ordered a coke.

"What about the rest of you?" the Sky Marshal asked. "If you can make it out of this court martial?"

"I want to be an aviator," Kai said.

"You look a bit young to join the Academy, let alone flight school," the Sky Marshal said.

"I'm sixteen."

"You can't join the Fleet until you're at least seventeen. That may cause problems. I hadn't realized you were so young. Major Westell just made up birthdates for those of you he couldn't find records for."

"If the records say I'm seventeen, then what's the problem?"

"Doctors could find out your true age," he said. "I'll have to talk to my JAGs. Well, what about the rest of you?"

Most of my squad told him their wishes, and then, with some hesitation, I gave him my answer.

"I want to follow in my father's footsteps. I want to command a starship, sir."

"A starship?" The Sky Marshal said, raising an eyebrow.

"Yes, sir."

"Your father would be proud."

"I believe so, sir."

"Good, and what about you?" the Sky Marshal asked, turning to Annabeth.

"I'm not exactly sure, sir," she said. "After London, I'm tired of fighting and don't really want to continue doing that."

"Well, Miss …"

"Annabeth Gauge, sir,"

"Well, Miss Gauge, if you don't join the Fleet, you may be forced back into the clutches of President O'Brien. There are lots of non-combat assignments in the Fleet. The first one that comes to mind is corpsman, or you could go the route of a Judge Advocate General and become a Fleet lawyer."

"A lawyer," Annabeth murmured. "My grandfather was a lawyer, and my mom always told me it would suit me."

"Well, you all have a wide band of options. Has the Academy and Boot Camp been explained to you yet?" The Sky Marshal asked.

"No, sir," I said.

The petty officer reappeared with our drinks and served them.

"Well, I'll explain it to you," the Sky Marshal said, relaxing into his seat and taking a sip from his drink. "You will all start at Boot Camp. At Boot Camp, you will either go in as a spaceman recruit or a midshipman. We train the recruits and the middies together, because only half of the midshipmen end up going to the Academy. The rest become either spacemen or CPOs. We just can't afford to have bad officers when we are on the brink of war. You will spend a month at Boot Camp, and, as long as you graduate Boot Camp as a midshipman, you will continue on to the Academy.

"At the Academy, you will be schooled for nine trimesters over the course of three years. After that, you will graduate as an ensign in the Solar Fleet and receive orders to your first duty station. That is, of course, as long as the war doesn't pop up in less than three years, at which point you may get your commission early and be sent out into the real navy.

"Except, of course, for Annabeth Gauge. If she does wish to become a JAG, she would have to go earth-side for schooling. We don't offer legal training at the Academy, besides the three week-legal officer course."

My heart jumped. I had always assumed Annabeth would be with me during our training. I glanced over at her and saw her nod.

"I sort of assumed that, sir," she said.

I wanted to talk to her, but I wasn't ready to interrupt the most powerful man in the solar system.

"We didn't quite do things by the book with you guys," the Sky Marshal said. "The papers that Andrus filled out are the commissioning paperwork. You will be sworn in as midshipmen as soon as I can get uniforms for you."

The Sky Marshal glanced down at his wrist and stood up. "I need to get onto the bridge. I'll see you when we dock." With that, the Sky Marshal left us alone.

I wanted to talk to Annabeth in private. I would have to wait to do that after we docked. Jenny and Richard started talking about

Boot Camp, and the rest of us joined in every once in a while, but my heart wasn't in it. I couldn't get my mind off of Annabeth and the fact that she would probably be leaving me.

"All hands, we are approaching Dalton Spaceways. If you wish to have a view of the station before we dock, please follow the blinking green lights to a view port."

I jumped. Who wouldn't want to see a space station? We followed the blinking green lights, and there was Dalton Spaceways. It was the most beautiful thing I had ever seen. The space station consisted of two giant wheels spinning slowly to create gravity. On the side of the station, in bright white lights, was written "Dalton Spaceways - Commercial Space Station." There must have been over a hundred ships docked at the many ports that dotted the central hub of the station, and there were many places where small ships appeared to be repairing or expanding the station.

"Wow," was all I managed to say.

"It doesn't have to rotate," Richard said. "Mr. Dalton just does that for effect. With Samuel Graves' invention of the gravity field, the station produces its own gravity without needing the centrifugal force created by the spinning.

"And no one is allowed in the second ring. DSI claims that it's an expansion to Dalton Spaceways that isn't quite ready to be opened yet, but I think its DSI's military base."

"DSI has a military?" I asked, confused.

"Yeah," Richard said. "It's called the Dalton Space Force."

"It couldn't be big enough to use up a whole ring of the station." Kai seemed unconvinced.

"Easily," Richard said. "It's estimated to be about ten thousand strong. It isn't a small force. DSF is the main reason that war hasn't broken out in orbit. Neither side is quite sure if Mr. Dalton is on their side, and his forces will easily tip the balance one way or the other."

"You mean he isn't a supporter of the Solar Fleet?"

"Most people believe he is, but he has never openly stated that, and UME personnel are allowed on the station. Dalton Space Industries is completely neutral."

We were approaching fast, so it wasn't long before all we could see was our docking berth. We headed back to the wardroom and waited for someone to collect us. A couple minutes later, the Sky Marshal came for us.

"Follow me," he said. "I've already got hotel rooms for you and reservations to the best restaurant on the station."

We followed him out of the ship, and I gasped when we entered the station. It was bustling with activity. I saw both UME and Solar Military uniforms in the mix, and each group pointedly ignored the other. I saw strange black uniforms that I didn't recognize, until I noticed "DSF" marked on a shoulder, and I figured they must be part of Dalton Space Force.

"The only thing that's missing is aliens," Kai muttered.

The Sky Marshal laughed. "Impressed then?"

"Oh yes, sir," we all said.

"Almek," The Sky Marshal said, as we continued through the station. "How will you handle the Academy?"

"What do you mean by that, sir?" I asked.

"You've been the commander of what, fifty people? How are you going to handle being the lowest on the totem pole?"

I smiled. "I won't like it, sir, but I'll have to adjust."

"That's what I like to hear …"

"Excuse me," a deep voice said in a commanding tone. I looked away from the Sky Marshal and saw four men in the black uniforms of Dalton Space Force.

"How may I help you boys?" the Sky Marshal asked.

The security man, a lieutenant by his shoulder boards, nodded to his handheld. "The people you are escorting, Sky Marshal. They tripped the facial recognition system. It says I have to escort them to Mr. Dalton immediately."

"Mr. Dalton knows of their presence here," the Sky Marshal said. It was obvious that he wasn't used to being treated like this by a lowly lieutenant.

"Sir," the lieutenant said persistently. "I have to escort these six," he said pointing to Jenny, Annabeth, Kai, Kris, Marian, and me. "And just them."

"Do you know who I am, son?" the Sky Marshal asked.

"Sky Marshal Bartholomew Kitt, of the Solar Fleet. With all due respect, sir, you are not in my chain of command."

The Sky Marshal shrugged, obviously giving up. Turning to us he said, "Meet me up at the Astrogator's Bar and Grill. I'm buying."

I nodded. "Thank you, sir. We'll be there." Then I turned to face the lieutenant, "Where to, Lieutenant?"

The lieutenant had visibly relaxed now that the Sky Marshal had backed down. "Follow me."

The three other Space Forcers formed up around my group of six. They all had drawn weapons and were scanning the crowd.

"Lieutenant, are the weapons really needed?" I asked

"Just following orders," he said, not looking back, but scanning the crowd with his weapon drawn. "I don't worry about the reasons."

I nodded, and we walked in silence. We finally reached the main tunnel, but instead of turning into it, we were led into a small lift labeled "restricted area." The man palmed the keypad, and we all climbed into the lift. The guards finally relaxed and holstered their guns. The ride was short, and we were soon in a large office area that was filled with people in the black of Dalton Space Force. It wasn't long before we were standing in front of a door that had two words printed in bold lettering: "Jack Dalton." Then beneath those two words it read: "Owner Dalton Space Industries, Commander-in-Chief Dalton Space Force."

If there was one man more powerful than the Sky Marshal, it would be Jack Dalton.

The lieutenant knocked, and we were ushered in.

I was expecting to see a man in his forties or fifties wearing the uniform of the Space Force or wearing a business suit. Instead I was facing a man who couldn't be more then twenty-five wearing jeans and a t-shirt that read: "Dalton Spaceways: Biggest Mall in the Solar System."

Mr. Dalton nodded at the lieutenant. "Thank you. You and your men will get a nice bonus for the extra duty. Dismissed."

The Space Forcers clicked their heels, saluted, and left the room, shutting the door behind them.

"Almek," Mr. Dalton said. "I sure am glad to see you. I was worried that idiot of a President would have you killed before you made it here. I would have sent down Blue Squadron to rescue you, but that would have caused a huge mess, and when I found out that Mike was handling it for us, we backed off. We were ready to come in if Captain Nine failed, though."

I was unsure of what to say.

"Excuse me, sir," Kris spoke up and asked what I was thinking. "Why would you want to save us?"

"I wasn't the one who wanted to save you," he said.

That statement had me even more baffled. Who else would want to save me? And who had that much influence on Jack Dalton to make him risk an intrasystem conflict. I wasn't that important. My dad had really good friends, and that was why Commodore Andrus and Captains Belnap and Nine were willing to risk so much for me, but who would be able to persuade Jack Dalton to rescue me and my ragtag gang of teenagers?

Then a strange, yet familiar, figure flickered into existence in front of me.

# Chapter 8
## Reunion

The figure standing before me was like nothing I had ever seen before … well, not quite. I had seen something very similar before, and that was a dog with a blue star on her forehead. Except this dog was standing on hind legs that looked more human than canine. Its body was covered in blonde fur, and it had a sash running from its left shoulder to its right hip. On its forehead was a star that was much smaller than Saph's star, but it was a five-point star, and it was the exact same shade of blue. I glanced to its arms, and saw that it had very well developed hands, with three fingers and an opposable thumb on each hand.

"Saph?" Jenny gasped.

"Not quite," the dog creature said. "I am Ardent, second in command of the Canid ship *Zochtil*."

"What?" I said, dumbfounded.

"I am Saph," another dog creature said, revealing herself. "Though my true name is Sonnel III of the Devellon line. I am High Alpha of the Canids."

"The Canids?"

"We are a race that has been driven to near extinction by the Draconians. To the best of my knowledge, my ship, *Zochtil,* is the only remaining Canid ship. We are here to aid you in your battle against the Draconians."

"Saph, we do want to defeat the Draconians, but we have to worry about the UME first … wait a second, how much did you help me in London?"

"A lot," she said. "Along with Ardent and the entire crew of the *Zochtil*."

"I thought you died," Marian said.

"It was an illusion. I needed to get back to my ship, and you were capable of escaping on your own."

I shook my head. It was hard to change my mental image of my dog Sapphire to one of the royal High Alpha Sonnel III. I had a million questions to ask, and I'm sure that the rest of my squad felt the same way.

However, before I could say anything, Sonnel raised her paw to silence any.

"Let me start from the beginning," she said. "The Canids made it into space three centuries ago. One century later, we made it to our closest moon. Half a century after that, we had built our first space colony. Another half century later, we started exploring the stars. Ten years after that we ran into the Draconians. They had only been exploring space for about as long as we had, but they had spent much more effort building weapons. They slaughtered our first four colonies before we had a chance to fight back. Then about three years into the war, they stopped fighting. That's when they encountered the Zarc. The Zarc were more technologically powerful than anything we have ever seen since then. However, they were a peaceful species and struggled to adapt to fighting. Within a decade, the Draconians had eliminated them, and they turned their attention back towards us. Now, however, the Draconians had an ally, the Passerines. We fought long and hard, until we discovered earth. Our home planet was already destroyed, and the fleet was scattered. We had been planning and waiting for the right moment to reveal ourselves. We were almost discovered when we rescued the crew of the *Mayflower,* but our cloaking technology is more advanced than the Draconians, so they couldn't find us. We followed the crew of the *Mayflower* carefully when they made it back to earth. I went on a recon mission to seek out the captain's son, to see if you would make a proper liaison. I became good friends with you over those years. I judged that you would make a good liaison and a good starship captain. And there you have the one-minute version of the history of my people."

"Wow," Annabeth said. "I think you answered about twenty questions and gave me another forty to ask."

Ardent laughed, or at least that's what I assume his short high-pitched barking meant.

I felt the same way Annabeth did. I had so many questions that were flooding my mind.

Finally, I decided on the simplest question that I wanted answered. "Why are you here?"

"Are you referring to being here with you, or being here with Jack Dalton?" Sonnel asked.

"Both, but first, why me?"

"We followed many of the *Mayflower* crew. We were trying to find someone whom we could help, someone who wasn't in the heart of the government. When my recon agents told me that you were in the slums of your planet, I left to join you and learn more about humans. I must say I did learn a lot from my time with you in London Proper. I haven't seen a race that is so violent to each other besides the Draconians, but that's a discussion for another day. I became attached to you and wanted to save you. Since that would have caused a nightmare, I recruited Jack to help out.

"As you know, we didn't end up rescuing you, since you managed to escape on your own. We have been trading technology with Jack for the past month. With the help of the Canids, Dalton Space Force will be able to take on the Draconian blockade ships."

"Why the Space Force and not the Fleet?" I asked, my pride in the Fleet coming through very strongly.

"To put it bluntly," she said. "The Space Force is about ten years ahead of the Fleet, and though the Force is smaller, it could easily defeat the Fleet."

"Now, now, Sonnel," Jack Dalton, said smiling. "You can't go around giving away the most closely guarded secrets of DSI."

"Soon," Sonnel said turning to him. "All of you humans will have to work together if you wish to defeat the Draconians. There can be no UME, no SF, and no DSF. There must be one united space navy."

"Bleck," Dalton said. "You make it sound like Marxism or something. We may cooperate, but we won't be 'one united space navy' as you put it. Dalton Space Force will always be a private military organization."

"Humans," Sonnel said, shaking her head.

Ardent stepped forward. "At any rate, we *are* working to unify you, or at least get you working together. The Solar Fleet is not ready to use the technology we could give them, and we are too small to work on bringing two separate fleets up to spec. We are working on the Space Force first and, once we are done, we'll work on bringing the Fleet up to spec with the help of Mr. Dalton. We want you to be our liaison with the Fleet."

There was silence in the room for a long time.

"Will you accept?" Sonnel asked.

"Of course!" I gasped.

"Good," Ardent said. "We will need a way of contacting you at all times."

"There won't be any way to do that," I said. "I don't believe we are allowed outside communication at Boot Camp."

Ardent laugh-barked. "We are very far ahead of you, remember? We are going to equip you with communication, but we don't have the time to do it now. Your Sky Marshal is already getting anxious."

"I'm sure he is. He wasn't happy about being overruled."

"The Sky Marshal is used to being a god," Dalton smiled. "Of course, he dislikes being overruled.

"I have a proposition for all of you. You are all in a lot of trouble with the PC and O'Brien. I can help. Join the Dalton Space Force, and I can protect you."

"I'll join," Kai said, without hesitation.

"I figured you would," Dalton nodded. "I have the forms right here." He handed a pad to Kai. "Just place your thumb at the bottom and you're in."

Kai did.

"What about the rest of you?"

"No, thanks," Jenny said and was soon echoed by the rest of the squad. We would tough out the court martial and continue on into the Solar Military.

"Well, Kai," Mr. Dalton said. "You're on leave until the rest of your friends head off wherever they decide to go. Then I want you to report to flight school."

"How did you know I wanted to be an aviator?" Kai asked.

Dalton smiled from ear to ear and said, "I am Jack Dalton." As if that explained everything. And I thought that it did.

"Okay," Dalton said. "I will have the lieutenant you met earlier escort you back here tomorrow afternoon, so that you can meet with Sonnel and Ardent again. Until then I want you to be armed at all times."

"We are technically prisoners," Annabeth said. "We aren't allowed to carry weapons."

"Look," Dalton said, leaning across his desk. "I know that O'Brien is trying get you killed before the court martial. He doesn't trust the Sky Marshal, and he's hiring assassins on the station. I've already arrested one man who was hunting you. I need you to be armed."

O'Brien was still after me? Would my life ever settle down? Probably not, I answered myself. Not if I join the military.

"I'll talk to the Sky Marshal."

"Good," Dalton said. "Dismissed."

"Good-bye, Almek," Sonnel said.

"It was a pleasure meeting all of you," I said. "And it's wonderful to see you're alive and well, Sonnel."

She smiled at me, and we left Dalton's office. We were met by the same four men who had escorted us there. They led us back through the offices and out to the main passage. I looked around the main passage and couldn't help thinking about Jack Dalton's shirt. Dalton Spaceways really was a giant mall. The four Space Forcers escorted us all the way to the Astrogator's Bar and Grill. We entered, and three of them stood as guards outside the door while the lieutenant followed us in.

I stopped him. "Are you on permanent assignment as body guards?"

"Yes," he said.

"Can I at least get your name?"

"John McFarland."

We found the Sky Marshal sitting with Commodore Andrus, Captain Belnap, and Richard Winters at a table in the corner talking and sipping beers. When Richard saw us, he looked happy to see us. He seemed a little uncomfortable with so much brass around.

"Finally," he said. "What did Mr. Dalton want you for?"

I had already decided on my cover story. I obviously couldn't tell him about Sonnel and the Canids.

"First, he tried to recruit us into the Space Force. He told us he could protect us and solve all of our problems with O'Brien."

"I bet he could," The Sky Marshal muttered.

"Kai accepted, but the rest of us are still thinking about it."

"Good," the Sky Marshal said. "Because my JAGs couldn't figure out how to handle the issue of Kai's age. So, that makes things much easier. What else did you discuss?"

"Then he told us that O'Brien has already hired one assassin, and he believes that there are more on the loose. Thus, the guards," I nodded back at Lieutenant McFarland.

"I was afraid of that. I can add a marine detachment to the Space Force guards."

"No," I said. "Four is enough … if we can carry weapons."

The Sky Marshal bit his lip in thought. "I'll need to get proof from Jack that you had an assassin on your tail, then I might be able to get the judge to allow you to be armed."

"On to another subject," I said. "What is the deal with Jack Dalton?"

"What do you mean?"

"He owns the largest company in the system, yet he wears jeans and t-shirts."

The Sky Marshal laughed. "I wondered that too when I first met the guy. It just seems to be his personality. He doesn't like to make a display. He knows that he is high and mighty, and that's good enough for him."

"Interesting," I said.

"Also," Kris said. "That guy seems really young."

"Yeah," The Sky Marshal nodded. "He's twenty-five. He started Dalton Space Industries when he was nineteen. He's got an interesting story. There's been a lot of biographies written about him. I recommend you read one sometime. Especially you, Kai, as he's going to be your Commander-in-Chief."

"So, should we read the biographies about you?" Annabeth asked, smiling.

The Sky Marshal laughed. "My life isn't anywhere near as interesting as Mr. Dalton's."

We chatted for the next hour while we ate dinner, which we heartily enjoyed since it was our first real meal since London Proper. When we finished eating, the Sky Marshal showed us to our hotel and said he would be there first thing in the morning to give us the verdict on the weapons.

"Almek," Annabeth said, pulling me aside before I entered my room. "I need to talk to you."

"Shoot," I said, leaning against the wall and crossing my arms.

"Not here," she said. "In private."

I turned to McFarland. "Is there a river up here somewhere?"

"Yes," he answered.

"Could you take us to it?"

"Only if the rest of your squad promises to stay here at the hotel."

"They will," I said.

Jenny nodded. She understood.

"Follow me," McFarland said.

One of the Space Forcers stayed behind, and McFarland led Annabeth and me to the nature preserve. He set up guards around us, then he backed up out of earshot. We sat down as we always did, with our arms wrapped around our knees.

"What's up?" I asked after a long silence.

"Almek," she took a deep breath. "It's time to call off our relationship."

I had been looking at the stream, but my head jerked around to her. She was still looking at the river. Her eyes were filled with sorrow, and I noticed tears forming in the corners of her eyes. My first reaction would have been to ask her if she was serious, but I could tell that she was. I wasn't sure what to say.

"Why?" I finally asked, lamely.

"Almek, you are going off to the Academy. You will be surrounded by hundreds of beautiful and smart girls. I'll be back earth-side at college, studying hard to be a JAG or maybe a corpsman. We will both be too busy for a long distance relationship."

"I'm willing to take the time, and you are both beautiful and smart, Annabeth."

"That's sweet Almek," she smiled weakly, as a tear slowly rolled down her cheek. I reached out to brush it away, but she stopped my hand. "I'm serious, Almek. Let's call it off."

"Annabeth, we still have weeks before we have to part ways, why can't we enjoy what time we have left?"

"Because it is time for both of us to get over each other. Let's use this time to become friends so that things won't be awkward when we see each other in the future."

"Why don't you want to follow the rest of us to the Academy?" I asked her.

"I'm sick of fighting, Almek. I'm tired of the killing. I know that fighting may be necessary to get out of this solar system, but I don't want to be the one doing the killing anymore. I have killed too much, and this is my chance to escape from it. It was one thing to fight for our survival in London Proper, but I don't want to make killing a profession."

I sighed. I understood how she felt. I wanted to quit fighting myself, but the desire to follow in my father's footsteps was stronger. I wanted to fulfill his dream of reaching the stars. I longed to captain a starship.

"I understand, Annabeth. I would love to put fighting behind me…"

"Get down!"

I spun around and flattened myself on the bank of the stream, as did Annabeth. I heard the all too familiar sound of a laser blast as it passed through foliage a couple of centimeters above me. I looked around but couldn't see the source of the blast, until all three of my guards started firing into a bush.

"McFarland!" I shouted. "Toss me your sidearm!"

He was using his rifle, and he glanced over at me.

"Now!"

He hesitated a second longer, then he unclipped the holster and tossed the gun to me. I checked the charge clip, flipped the safety off, got up from the bank, and ran to a tree. I saw return fire coming from the bush and sprinted to the next tree. So I could flank him.

I dashed from tree to tree, and then I was behind him. But no one was there. It was just a small rifle-sized autogun. I aimed my automatic at it and fired two shots: one at its brain and the other at its base. The autogun stopped firing.

"Lieutenant McFarland!" I called out.

"Yes."

"It was an autogun."

McFarland swore loudly, "So the guy got away!"

"How did you spot him?"

"He tripped my facial recognition software, and I assumed he was after you."

"So, do you have a name?"

"No, the system just pinged him as dangerous, and I told you to duck. He was carrying a sniper rifle, I didn't notice the autogun, though."

"Wow."

"Well," McFarland said. "You two are going back to your hotel." He held out his hand, and I returned his sidearm.

"That's a nice gun."

"Thanks. You're a good shot. Not many people could knock out the brain like that."

I nodded, then went back to Annabeth.

"Sorry our conversation was interrupted."

She shook her head. "It just serves to prove my point. I don't want to live this kind of life anymore. It's time for a change."

"Believe me, I understand."

Annabeth just nodded and leaned in to give me a kiss on my cheek.

"You aren't making it any easier," I laughed.

"Let's move!" McFarland shouted at us.

We followed him out of the preserve and went back to the hotel. I was about to lie down to sleep when I realized how filthy I was. I looked down at my clothes, which were tattered and torn like all the clothes I owned. I didn't have any clean clothes to change into, but I saw that problem had already been solved when I opened the door of the closet. Inside was a rack full of clothes from jeans to a suit.

I fully enjoyed the first shower I had taken in almost five years. I really scrubbed down, and, after maybe an hour, I felt truly clean again.

I lay down but couldn't fall asleep. I was awake for at least another hour, thinking about Annabeth and me. We had known each other for two years and had been "dating" a whole year. It wasn't going to be easy to forget about all the time we had spent together. In fact, if it hadn't been for Annabeth, I never would have made it through my time as squad leader in London Proper. Thinking back, it was amazing how much stuff had been crammed into the last thirty-six hours or so. I was finally overcome by pure exhaustion and lost consciousness.

# Chapter 9
## Clash of The JAGs

I woke up to the buzzing of the doorbell. It was Lieutenant McFarland.

"Yeah?" I asked.

"The Sky Marshal is here to see you."

"Okay. Just let me get ready."

It wasn't long before I was with the Sky Marshal again.

"I'm glad to see that you found the clothes Chief Voyage brought over."

"Thank you, sir," I said. "It appears that my squad and I owe you a lot."

"Don't be counting debts just yet," the Sky Marshal said. "You still have a court martial to wade through."

"So, what's the verdict on the weapons?"

"The judge said yes, especially after the assassination attempt, though at first he just wanted to lock you up in the brig."

"Well, I'm glad you talked him out of that one."

Then Richard Winters joined us. His arm no longer had the laser burn.

"Is your arm doing better?" I asked.

"Yeah, it is." He smiled. "It's good to see you're still alive. The assassination attempt was all over the news this morning."

"They didn't get me this time, at least, and once I have a gun, I'll try to keep it challenging for them."

We waited for the rest of my squad to gather in the hotel's lobby and had a quick breakfast. Then we went to buy some equipment. As usual, we were followed closely by McFarland and his men. At the firearm store, I felt like a kid in a candy store. I hadn't seen so many new guns at once in years. I couldn't help but want to have the gun with the newest whistles and gadgets, but since I wasn't paying,

I turned it down. Until McFarland walked over and handed me a credit chit.

"This is from Mr. Dalton."

I ran it through the machine at the store and saw that Mr. Dalton had been very generous. I quickly bought the gun I wanted and waited for each of the others to get one, which didn't take long. We all stuck to handguns, except for Jenny who picked a nice, long-barreled automatic rifle, which she slung over her back.

Once we had the guns, we proceeded to a computer store. I had been out of the computer world for so long, I wasn't quite sure what we needed, but Richard solved that problem for us rather quickly. He knew everything about every computer in the store, and he showed us which ones were the best, and what apps were the best. We all picked a computer and loaded it up. Now that we were back in the real world, we wanted the gadgets we had been used to as kids.

"Okay," the Sky Marshal said. "Now that we've gotten the shopping out of the way, can we do something useful?"

"Sure."

"We have a JAG to see. All except for you, Mr. Winters."

"Okay, then," Richard said. "You've all got my number, so just give me a buzz when you want me to show you how to use your gadgets."

The Sky Marshal pressed a couple of buttons on his wrist computer, and we headed off again. Soon we were standing at the entrance to the Solar Military offices. We left McFarland and his men outside and were led through numerous passageways until we reached the JAG offices. We had barely stepped in when we were jumped by a young female JAG.

"Excuse me, Sky Marshal, but why are these traitors armed?"

Jenny made a threatening gesture towards her rifle, and the JAG flinched.

"Watch it," I hissed, my own hand hovering near my sidearm.

"Ah, Lieutenant *Junior* Grade Michelle Silver," the Sky Marshal said. "You aren't up to date. The Judge okayed these weapons himself."

The JAG looked surprised. "Why?"

"Because your client has hired assassins to kill these young midshipmen."

This time the woman looked extremely offended. "Are you accusing the President of hiring assassins?"

"Yes," the Sky Marshal said. "And I'll prove it, some time."

"You never will. See you all in court!"

"JAGs," the Sky Marshal muttered under his breath, as Silver walked away.

"Hey," Annabeth said.

The Sky Marshal just laughed and led us to the office of Commander Jon Schmidt, Judge Advocate General Corps.

"Come in," the commander said. "You must be my clients."

"Yes, sir," I said, delivering a sharp, precise salute.

"Thanks," he said. "Now, let me start off by saying this. I think we've got the case in the bag. We have some tough spots to smooth over, but very few people in the SF like O'Brien, so they won't be overly anxious to listen to the speeches of O'Brien's pet JAG."

"What about our papers?" Annabeth asked.

The JAG sighed heavily. "They won't make things easier, that is for sure."

"Will we win?" Kris asked.

"I think we will. ..." His computer chimed. He turned to face the screen, his eyes rapidly moving across it. "I may have spoken prematurely," he muttered. "Six of the twelve members of the court are in O'Brien's pocket. We won't be convincing neutral officers."

"Can't you object?" Annabeth asked.

"Normally, yes, but this is a very complicated and unique case, and I'm sure that raising objections wouldn't do any good. I have already spent hours arguing with Michelle over Article 37."

"O'Brien hasn't dropped that?" the Sky Marshal asked.

"In some ways, that is his strongest asset, but you are the Sky Marshal. Anything you do influences the way officers think. The question remains, is it legal? Article 37 relates to illegally influencing members of the court."

"I see Silver's point, but what does she want to do? Have them tried by the UME or, better yet, the Draconians?"

Schmidt laughed. "She would probably prefer that. Well, I need to drill all of you." Thus it began. Schmidt hammered us with question after question, and by the time he was through, I felt like we had just been in front of the Spanish Inquisition, or its Draconian equivalent. Finally, we were interrupted by a knock on the door. It was Lieutenant McFarland.

"Excuse me, sirs," Lieutenant McFarland said. "But Mr. Dalton is requesting the presence of Almek and company."

I could see the Sky Marshal's annoyance with Jack Dalton just by his posture.

"Will you excuse us?" I asked the Sky Marshal and Schmidt.

"We wouldn't want to keep you from seeing Mr. Dalton, now, would we?" the Sky Marshal asked.

I smiled. "Thanks, it's good to know you're on such good terms with the most powerful man in the solar system."

The Sky Marshal glowered at me as we exited the office. Lieutenant McFarland led us back to Mr. Dalton's office, but, before he knocked, he turned to me.

"Excuse me," he said. "I must ask. How does a not-yet-sworn-in midshipman gain the attention of the two most powerful people on this side of the war?"

"It's all about networking," I said, patting him on the shoulder.

McFarland was obviously still confused, but he let us in anyway.

Mr. Dalton was dressed as he had been the day before, except that his shirt read: "Which will it be? Plymouth Plantation or

Plymouth Station?" In the center of his t-shirt was a big picture of Plymouth Station. I still couldn't quite understand this guy.

As soon as McFarland shut the door behind us, both Sonnel and Ardent appeared in the room with us. We quickly exchanged greetings, then settled into our seats and started talking shop.

"Okay," I said. "Just how are we supposed to communicate with you from Boot Camp?"

Mr. Dalton looked over at Ardent.

"Well," Ardent began. "Its fairly simple: just use an implant."

"A what?" I asked, confused. I had heard of implants before but wasn't sure what he meant. Anytime before when researchers or inventors had tried brain implants, the person with the implant had died.

"An implant," Ardent tapped his head. "A computer strapped directly to your brain."

"Won't medical scans show the implant?" Annabeth asked.

"No. This implant will have a small cloaking shield which will allow it to remain undetected for at least three years."

"How safe is it?"

Ardent waved his paw towards Mr. Dalton.

"Well," Mr. Dalton said. "McFarland was the first person to receive an implant. Has he ever mentioned his facial recognition software?"

"Yeah," I said, still confused.

"It's all in the implant. He's had the implant for the past week. There are twenty others who have implants also. One of them is me. I obviously trust the technology. It is already revolutionizing the Space Force, and once everyone has an implant, the Space Force will be ten times more effective."

"Cool!" Jenny said.

"I'm in," I said.

"Are you kidding me?" Annabeth asked. "Do you know how much easier school will be with this? I am so in with this, too!"

Mr. Dalton got up, led us out of his office and down many flights of stairs to a hospital.

"We'll have to do this one at a time, so who is first?"

"I am," I said.

"Okay, follow me."

He led me to an operating room where four Canids waited for me.

\*\*\*

I awoke with a jolt and saw a transparent reboot symbol in the lower left corner of my vision. It showed a paw with a short string of what I assumed was Canid lettering. Shortly, the lettering adapted to English, and I saw "Cloud Computers" printed across the paw. Then another message flashed in the corner of my vision.

*Human adapted Cloud Implant V1.1.*

I briefly wondered what had been wrong with the original version. Then another message flashed in the center of my vision.

*Can you read this? Think "yes" or "no."*

*Good, do you prefer written messages or oral?*

Then I no longer saw the string of words, but heard a pleasant female voice.

*Is this voice suitable?* I heard inside my own head. I thought, *yes*, back to it.

After about an hour of this type of exchange, my implant was fully configured, and then the tutorial started running. Two hours later, I thought I had a vague idea of how to use it but only a very vague idea. It was incredible how many things the implant could be used for. The advantages for a combat situation were obvious. This *would* revolutionize warfare.

I checked my implant and discovered that it was already 1700. The Sky Marshal would be getting anxious. My first thought was to contact him over my implant, and I had already started searching for his implant code when I realized he didn't have one. I contacted Mr. Dalton instead.

*Yes,* he said over his 'plant.

*How much longer will it be for the rest of my squad?*

*One more hour,* he replied. *All we have left is Kris, but Kris won't be ready to leave until about 2100.*

*The Sky Marshal will be anxious by then.*

*He doesn't like me very much does he?* Mr. Dalton asked.

*No, not really.*

By 2100, we were ready to go. We met up with McFarland at the entrance of Space Force headquarters.

*So you all have implants now?* McFarland asked.

*Yep,* I said.

*How are you guys so well connected?* he marveled.

"You wouldn't believe me," I said. We walked in silence to the hotel, though that no longer meant that we weren't talking. We were all testing our implants and randomly calling each other. We were half way to the hotel when my wrist computer went off. I answered it. It was the Sky Marshal, and he looked very stressed.

"Where have you been?" he said. "I've been trying to contact you for the past three hours, and you never responded."

"I never received your calls, sir," I said.

*The hospital doesn't allow calls from non-hospital phones to get through,* McFarland informed me.

"I must have been in a location where I couldn't receive calls, sir."

"Obviously. I swear I'm going to hurt that J…"

"You may be about to say something about the owner of the station in front of four of his sailors."

The Sky Marshal finally smiled. "I suppose that might not be helpful," he said. "I've got bad news for the six of you."

"What?" I asked cautiously.

"Your court martial has been moved up."

"To when?"

"Tomorrow at noon."

"What!" I said incredulously. "Is Commander Schmidt ready?"

"No," he said. "He has a case prepared, but he says he's not ready yet."

"Well, he has to be ready."

"Which is why he needs to spend more time talking to you and your friends."

"Okay," I said. "We'll be at his office shortly."

"No," the Sky Marshal said. "Over dinner, it's already past 2100."

"Okay," I nodded. "The Astrogator's Grill again?"

"Yeah."

"Did you get that, Lieutenant?" I asked.

"Yep," McFarland said. "Back to the Astrogator's Grill."

When we arrived at the restaurant, we found the Sky Marshal, Commander Schmidt, and Richard Winters.

"Why are you here, Richard?" I asked him after I had saluted the other two officers.

"I've been called as a witness," he said.

"Why?"

Schmidt answered that question. "I'm not sure, but I assume it has something to do with your trip in Global Transport XK-12."

"Great," I muttered. "Well, let's get this over with…"

So, the drilling resumed. After two hours, Schmidt left to work on the case alone, and we were left with the Sky Marshal.

"There is one thing left that we have to do," the Sky Marshal said. "I want to have you sworn in and in uniform before the court martial begins."

"Why?" Annabeth asked.

"Schmidt thought that wearing uniforms would leave a better impression than just showing up in civvies."

"Logical," I said.

"So reveille will be at 0500. You can't sleep in tomorrow."

# Chapter 10
## The Court Martial Begins

The day had started out simply enough. We had all woken up at 0500 as the Sky Marshal instructed and went down to the lobby to find that the Sky Marshal had arranged for a small breakfast for us. We ate quickly, not talking much. We were nervous about the upcoming court martial.

As soon as we finished breakfast, the Sky Marshal took us over to the Fleet Exchange, and we quickly found uniforms for all of us. The Sky Marshal found the proper insignia for us to wear, a single small star. We left the FX, and the Sky Marshal led us to his local office.

"Are you ready to take the oath?" he asked seriously.

"Yes," we all said.

"Then repeat after me. I, Bartholomew Kitt, do solemnly swear (or affirm) that I will support and defend the Constitution of the Presidential Council against all enemies, foreign and domestic; that I will bear true faith and allegiance to the same; and that I take this obligation freely, without any mental reservation or purpose of evasion; and that I will well and faithfully discharge the duties of the office on which I am about to enter. So help me God."

After we had all repeated the last sentence of the oath, the room fell silent. We all knew that this was a historic occasion. Finally, Kai spoke up behind us.

"We've now all accomplished what we came here for, to join the military. Now, if we can just manage to honorably stay in it."

I turned to face him and noticed the contrast in his dress blacks and my dress whites.

"This isn't quite the way I had imagined things would go down," I said.

"Ditto for me," Richard said. He, too, had been sworn in. The Sky Marshal had said that he wanted Richard to be in uniform when he was called to the stand.

"Well," the Sky Marshal said. "Now for you Spaceman Taggart."

The Sky Marshal then swore in Kris as a spaceman recruit.

\*\*\*

"All rise for the military judge!" the bailiff called out.

We all stood as the military judge entered the room.

Once the military judge sat down, he spoke, "This Article 39 (a) session is called to order. You may be seated."

Lieutenant Silver stood up. "This court-martial is convened by general court-martial convening order 0312, Commander, Solar Fleet, copies of which have been furnished to the military judge, counsel, and the accused.

"The Charges were preferred by President Charles O'Brien, a person subject to the Code as Accuser and was sworn before a commissioned officer of the Solar Military authorized to administer oaths.

"The charges were served on the accused on April 20, 2183.

"The accused and the following persons detailed to the court-martial are present: Admiral Malik, Vice-Admiral Gardner, Commodore Morring, Commodore Young, Commodore Kelly..." the JAG finished listing the members of the court martial then continued, "Captain Griffith, Commander Schmidt, Lieutenant Junior Grade Silver."

"Bailiff," Judge Griffith said. "Please inform the members that they may enter the court room."

The bailiff nodded and went to a side door. He cracked it open, then stood aside. "All rise for the members of the court martial."

We all rose as the twelve members entered, and Admiral Malik nodded towards the military judge.

"You may be seated," the judge said. "Continue, trial counsel."

Lieutenant Silver walked up to the members' table. "I have been detailed to this court-martial by order of Charles O'Brien, President of the United States and Assistant Chair of the Presidential Council. I am qualified and certified under Article 27 (b) and sworn under Article 42 (a). I have not acted in any manner which might tend to disqualify me in the court-martial."

Commander Schmidt stood. "I have been detailed to this court-martial by order of the Solar Fleet Judge Advocate General's office. I am qualified and certified under Article 27 (b) and sworn under Article 42 (a). I have not acted in any manner which might tend to disqualify me in the court-martial."

"All counsel appear to have the requisite qualifications, and all personnel required to be sworn have been sworn," the military judge said.

We were all sitting at an elongated table with Commander Schmidt and his aide at the end of the table. Then the judge turned to face us. "Commodore Andrus, Captain Belnap, Cadet Thomas, Midshipmen Manning, Kade, Gauge, and Spaceman Recruit Taggart, you have the right to be represented in this court-martial by Commander Schmidt, your detailed military counsel.

"You may be represented by military counsel of your selection, if the counsel you request is reasonably available. If you are represented by military counsel of your own selection, you will lose the right to have Commander Schmidt continue to help in your defense.

"In addition, you have the right to be represented by a civilian lawyer. A civilian lawyer would have to be provided by you, at no expense to the Solar Military.

"If you are represented by a civilian lawyer, you may keep your military counsel on the case to assist your civilian lawyer, or you may be represented solely by your civilian lawyer. Do you understand your options?"

"Yes, we understand," Commodore Andrus said, speaking for all of us.

"Commander Schmidt, do you perceive any conflicts of interest in your representation of the accused?" the military judge asked Schmidt.

"No, sir, I do not."

"Whom do you want to represent you, Commodore Andrus and company?"

"We choose to keep the military counsel detailed to us by Admiral Walling."

The judge continued, "I have been detailed to this court by Admiral Walling, the Judge Advocate General of the Solar Fleet. I am certified in accordance with Article 26 (b) and sworn in accordance with Article 42 (a) of the Uniform Code of Military Justice. I am not a witness or otherwise ineligible under Article 26 (d). I am not aware of any matters that would provide a basis for challenge."

"The President has no challenge against the military judge," Silver said.

"The defense has no challenge against the military judge," Schmidt said.

The judge then turned to face us again, "Commodore Andrus and company, do you understand that you have the right to be tried by a court martial made up of members. If you wish to be tried by a court-martial composed of members, two-thirds of the members, voting by secret written ballot, must concur in any finding of guilty. And if you are found guilty, two-thirds of the members, again voting by secret ballot, must concur in a sentence. Do you understand this option?"

"Yes, we understand."

"Do you also understand that you may request in writing, or orally, to be tried in the court martial before me alone, and that if I approve your request, no members will be present, and I alone will decide whether you are guilty, and, if so, I will decide your sentence?"

"We understand."

"Commodore Andrus, by which type of court martial do you wish to be tried?"

"We wish to be tried by the members."

"Very well," the judge said. "The accused will now be arraigned."

Silver nodded to the judge, then looked at the members, "All parties, the military judge, the members, and the accused have been furnished with a copy of the charges and specifications. Does the accused wish them read?"

"The accused does not wish the charges to be read," Commander Schmidt said.

"Understood. I have read the charge sheet, convening order, and the amending orders," the military judge said. "Commodore Andrus and company, what is your plea?"

"We all plead not guilty to all charges and specifications," Commodore Andrus said.

The military judge nodded, "The trial counsel may now make an opening statement."

Lieutenant Silver stood up, "The United States of America charges Commodore Andrus and Captain Belnap with Article 94 in relation to mutiny and sedition, Article 90 in relation to willfully disobeying a superior commissioned officer, and Article 84 in relation to unlawfully accepting the appointment of Almek Manning and company. Commodore Andrus did not have the right to disobey the President's order, to accept the appointment of Almek Manning to midshipman, nor to unlawfully remove Almek Manning and company from the White House. Commodore Andrus and Captain Belnap should be found guilty of all charges and specifications.

"The United States of America also charges Almek Manning and company with Article 83 in relation to knowing false representation on their applications. Also they are charged with treason, espionage, and spying. The United States of America asserts that all of these men and women should be found guilty of all charges and specifications."

Silver sat down, while the military judge turned to face Commander Schmidt, "Will the defense now make an opening statement?"

"Yes, your honor," Schmidt said, standing up and facing the members of the court martial. "The defense intends to prove that Commodore Andrus and Captain Belnap were acting properly when they rescued Midshipman Almek Manning from his unlawful imprisonment, and that Commodore Andrus was in no way trying to incite mutiny or sedition. Also, Commodore Andrus had it within his power to accept Midshipman Manning and company's applications. Likewise, the defense will prove that Midshipman Almek Manning and his associates have no intent to commit treason or espionage, nor to spy, nor have they ever participated in any such activities against the Presidential Council. As such, the defense intends to show that all of these loyal officers in the Solar Fleet should be found innocent of all charges and specifications under the Uniform Code of Military Justice."

"You may now proceed, Lieutenant Silver," the judge said.

"I would like to present my first piece of evidence." Silver pulled out a pad and read, "'Executive Order by the President of the United States, Charles O'Brien. Almek Manning is hereby declared to be guilty of high treason, espionage, and spying.'

"This executive order gives President O'Brien the right to sentence Almek Manning to death. He was in the process of carrying out this lawful order when Commodore Andrus illegally removed him from federal custody."

Commander Schmidt stood up again, facing the judge. "I request that Midshipman Almek Manning be given the respect of a commissioned officer in the Solar Fleet, and be henceforth called by his title of midshipman."

"Judge," Silver said. "We have not confirmed that he is a legal midshipman."

"Lieutenant, your statement is incorrect," the judge said. "You have not brought forward to the court information demonstrating that he is not a legal midshipman. Do you intend to bring forth such evidence at this time?"

"No, sir," Silver said. "Not at this time, though I do reserve the right to return to this subject at a later point."

"Please, until otherwise proven unlawful, call Midshipman Manning by his title," the judge said.

"Yes, sir," Silver said. "I will now call to the stand the President of the United States of America and Assistant Chairman of the Presidential Council."

The military judge then swore in the President.

"Mister President," Silver said. "Do you have the power to sentence someone to death under executive order?"

"Yes, Lieutenant, that power was given to me under the fifty-seventh amendment to the Constitution of the United States of America."

"Do you have the right to give an officer of the Solar Military stationed in the United States an order?"

"Yes, I do."

"What was the exact wording of your order to Commodore Andrus?"

"I told Commodore Andrus, that he was not to go anywhere near Almek Manning…"

"Objection!" Schmidt said. "You are to refer to Midshipman Manning by his rank."

"The objection is irrelevant," Silver said. "I asked him for the exact wording of his order."

"Objection overruled," the military judge said.

Silver nodded, "You may continue Mister President."

"Until after Manning's execution. I then instructed him to report to his duty post, which was the USS *Lincoln*."

"Did he obey your order?"

"No, he never showed up at the quarterdeck of the *Lincoln*, but instead he met with other officers in the Solar Fleet and a small squad of former Solar Marines and kidnapped Manning and the other UME spies."

"Objection!" Schmidt shouted. "Address Midshipman Manning by his title."

"Objection sustained," the military judge said.

"Sir, the witness was speaking his own thoughts not mine."

"Caution your witness, Lieutenant," the military judge said.

Silver nodded, then turned to Schmidt. "You may now cross-examine the witness."

"Mister President," Schmidt said, standing up and walking over to O'Brien. "Did you know that Midshipman Manning was in the Solar Fleet when you sentenced him to death?"

"No, I did not, and to my knowledge, their applications were not created until ten minutes or so after I issued the order."

"I will return to that point later," Schmidt said. "Did you have any proof of the charges you laid against him?"

"Under the fifty-seventh amendment, I need no proof during times of war."

"So, you didn't have any proof?"

"I do not wish to answer the question."

"You must," Schmidt said coolly.

"I plead the fifth."

"The fifth amendment only relates to self-incrimination, Mister President. Please answer the question," the judge said before Commander Schmidt could reply. "Continue Commander Schmidt."

"Would you like me to repeat the question?" Schmidt asked.

"No," O'Brien said. "I have no proof at this time, however …"

"That is enough, thank you. If you had known that Midshipman Manning was an officer in the Solar Fleet, would you still have sentenced him to death?"

"Objection!" Silver said, jumping out of her seat. "The defense is asking the witness a hypothetical question."

"Objection sustained," the judge said. "Rephrase your question Commander Schmidt."

Schmidt nodded, "Mister President, now that you know that Midshipman Manning is a member of the Solar Fleet, will you withdraw you executive order?"

"No. I still believe that the order is correct. Almek … Midshipman Manning is guilty of treason and espionage."

Schmidt asked President O'Brien a couple additional questions.

"Do the members have any questions for this witness?" the military judge asked.

"I do," Commodore Morring said. "Mister President, you knew Midshipman Almek Manning previously, did you not?"

"I did. Not well, but he was aboard the *Mayflower* with me."

"What were you impressions of him at that time."

"Objection!" Silver shouted.

"I would like to answer the question," O'Brien said.

"I withdraw my objection," Silver nodded towards O'Brien.

"A person can change a lot after being consigned to London Proper. I knew him when he was eleven. A lot can happen in seven years."

Commodore Morring nodded thoughtfully and recorded a note on her pad.

Silver brought forward a handful of witnesses who confirmed that Commodore Andrus did not return to his duty post, and that he met with others from the *Mayflower.*

"I am now ready to present my next item of evidence: forging the Midshipmen's applications to the Solar Fleet." Silver pulled out twelve pads, and gave one to each of the members. "You will find displayed on these pads the first item in question: the application of Midshipman Annabeth Gauge."

I glanced sharply over at her, but her eyes were focused on Silver.

"We know that there was once a person by the name of Annabeth Gauge, who lived in Germany before the Civil War. That is the extent of our knowledge. I would now like to call Midshipman Annabeth Gauge to the stand."

She turned to Commander Schmidt. "Should I go?" she asked in a whisper.

Commander Schmidt stood. "At this time, I do not want any of my clients on the stand."

"Understood," Silver said. She didn't seem surprised. "I would like to present the next item of evidence."

She pointed to the video screen on the wall directly opposite the members of the court martial. A video started playing. It showed my squad in the holding cell at the White House. It played for a couple minutes. Then the secret service man came in, holding our applications. We exchanged a couple of sharp words, and then we thumbed the documents. The secret service man left, and the video ended.

"That was the moment that Midshipman Annabeth Gauge thumbed her application. Before that she had never seen it, and yet…"

"Objection," Schmidt said. "That is speculation."

"Lieutenant Silver, confine your speculation to your closing statement," the military judge instructed.

"I will request once more to have Midshipman Gauge on the stand, to rebut my statement," Silver said.

"The answer is still 'no,'" Schmidt said.

"I would like to submit three more applications as evidence, the applications of Midshipman Jennifer Kade, Spaceman Recruit Kristine Taggart, and Cadet Marian Thomas. I would also like to request the subpoena of retired Major Thomas Westell, the secret serviceman in the video."

"Okay then," the military judge said, sighing. "My clerk will issue a subpoena for retired Major Westell. The court martial will be adjourned until 0900 hours tomorrow morning." He banged his gavel, and we all stood up.

I glanced over at Annabeth, "Well, now, JAG in training, what did you think?"

"I don't even know what to think. Well, okay, I do think that being a JAG is going to be very hard, but very satisfying."

I turned to face Commander Schmidt. "Well, Commander?"

He wore the facial expression of a man about to face a firing squad. "I had hoped she wouldn't call Major Westell," he muttered.

"Will that cost us our careers?" Kris asked.

"The case has certainly become tougher," he said, looking glum. "And yes, it may cost you your careers."

"Well," Andrus said, also looking depressed. "Can I buy you all dinner? The Sky Marshal and Mr. Dalton have had your ear for so long, I bet you would enjoy the simple company of a commodore."

I laughed, and it was only then that I realized Andrus had done so much for us, but I hadn't even properly thanked him. I hadn't even seen him since my first dinner on Dalton Spaceways.

"How about letting me treat," I said. "You are, after all, the person responsible for saving my life. I can at least pay for your dinner, right?"

"Sure," Andrus said, smiling. "That sounds like a fair trade."

I shook my head at him and led everyone out the door. At the exit, we were joined by Kai, Richard, Lieutenant McFarland, and his three men. I quickly scanned through the restaurants listed in my implant and picked one that seemed appropriate for the occasion.

"Ever been to the Spaceman's Asteroid?" I asked.

"Nope," Andrus said. "It's a bar that is normally reserved for JOs, but if a JO is buying, a senior officer like myself wouldn't be looked at too critically."

We ate dinner, then had our choice of beers afterwards. I tried persuading McFarland to at least have a bite of an appetizer, but he wouldn't eat anything. We discussed the court martial for a couple hours. Finally, tired of talking about the legal matters, we headed back to our respective rooms. That night, I dreamed about the assault of the UME base, and I lived it through the eyes of those who had fallen there: Kate, Alan, Ryan, and even other members who had stayed outside the gates to try and distract the UME forces. It was a horrible dream, and I woke up in a cold sweat at 0500 hours.

I shook myself and got into the 'fresher. I set the jets for a hard needle shower and tried to relax. I tried to let the water rinse out all of the pain of thinking about those who had fallen. I always hated it when I dreamed about a squad member dying.

It was still another fifteen minutes before the rest of the squad would be up, so I went down to the lobby, pulled up a chair, and started reading a space yarn I had picked up. It had been so long since I had read any fiction. It was good, but so unbelievable, at least until I thought about the past couple days of my life. I was soon joined by Jenny and Kai. We sat down to breakfast the Sky Marshal had convinced the hotel to prepare for us at reveille.

On the station, waking up at 0500 wasn't hard at all. As long as I went to bed by 2200, I could get eight hours of sleep because Dalton Spaceways operated on a twenty-five hour day. Jack Dalton just happened to think an extra hour was useful, and he could do whatever he wanted.

# Chapter 11
## Verdict

The military judge banged his gavel. "I now call this article 39 (a) court martial to order. Lieutenant Silver, have you found Major Westell?"

"Yes, I have, and I would like to call him to the stand."

The secret serviceman who had written the applications walked up to the stand and was sworn in.

"Major Westell," Silver began. "Did you write the applications for these midshipmen?" Silver said, pointing at us.

"Yes, ma'am."

"How did you know the birthdate of Midshipman Gauge?"

Major Westell hesitated.

"I remind you that you are under oath."

"I don't need you to remind me, Lieutenant," the Major barked back, sounding like a CO chastising a junior officer.

"Answer the question, Major," Judge Griffith said.

"I rolled dice," he said.

"Can you explain?" Silver said.

"I was able to guess the year based on their looks," the major said glumly. "But the day and month I just made up by rolling dice. I rolled dice rather than writing down whatever came to mind to reduce the chance that there might be a pattern in the dates."

"So you deliberately forged legal documents?"

"Yes, ma'am."

"Were you following orders when you forged those documents?"

"Yes, and no," the major said. "Commodore Andrus asked me to make out the applications for these midshipmen, but as I am no longer in the Solar Military I did not have to obey such an order."

"However, he does outrank you, so the desire to obey him is strong. The United States does not wish to press charges against you. Your witness, commander."

Schmidt stood up slowly, and walked over to the witness stand.

"Major," Schmidt said. "Do you see any way that these midshipmen could have filled out their own applications?"

"Objection!"

"I contest," Schmidt said. "As the person who created the documents, he had to have a reason for filling them out."

"Objection overruled, Silver," the judge said.

"Shall I repeat the question?"

"No," Major Westell said. "For there to be any chance of these applications being useful, they had to be executed before the executive order was signed. If I didn't act quickly, it would have been too late to help these innocent midshipmen."

"Do you consider what you did to be morally wrong?"

"No, sir," he said. "According to the UCMJ, what I did was technically wrong, but was it morally wrong? Not in the slightest. I acted to protect teenagers who were about to be sentenced to death to protect the ambition of an egotistical politician."

"Thank you. That is all."

Silver got up and approached the stand, "Major, how certain are you that these midshipmen are who they say they are?"

He seemed startled by the question. "Why wouldn't they be?"

"I'm the one asking the questions."

"I just assumed they were who they said they were. Why wouldn't they be?"

"They are being tried for spying," Silver stated. "I have no further questions for this witness."

"Members?" the judge asked.

"Why do you believe that these midshipmen are not guilty?" a commodore asked him.

"Objection, opinion."

"Sustained. Do you wish to rephrase?"

"Major, you were just retired from President O'Brien's secret service, is that correct?" the commodore asked.

"Yes, sir."

"So as a member of the secret service, were you trained to detect enemy agents?"

"Yes, sir."

"Based on your professional experience, do you believe that these officers are or were engaged in espionage or spying?"

"No, sir."

"Thank you, that is all."

"Silver, call your next witness."

"I would like to call Midshipman Richard Winters to the stand."

Richard gave us a small smile as he walked past our seats. He sat down and was sworn in.

"Midshipman Winters were you aboard the Global Transport ship XK-12 on the day it was hijacked by Commodore Andrus?"

"Y…"

"Objection!" Schmidt said. "Commandeered, not hijacked!"

"Do you have proof that this was done under the auspices of the Fleet?"

"My client is a Commodore and, as such, he can commandeer a civilian ship as deemed necessary for a military operation," he said quoting regulations.

"Objection sustained," the judge said. "Restate your question."

"Midshipman Winters were you aboard the Global Transport ship XK-12 on the day it was commandeered by Commodore Andrus?" Silver restated.

"Yes."

"What did you do?"

"I staged a mutiny and, in the process, wound up getting a hole in my arm from a laser blast."

"Who shot you?"

"Midshipman Manning."

"So he caused you bodily harm?"

"Objection," Schmidt said, almost lazily. "Trial counsel is leading the witness."

"Sustained, please restate."

"I have no further questions."

Schmidt stood up and, without moving from behind the bar, asked one question, "What is your relationship with Almek Manning?"

"Objection, irrelevant."

"Your honor," Schmidt said. "I am trying to use Midshipman Winters as a character witness."

"Overruled. Continue, Commander."

"Thank you. Please answer the question, Midshipman."

"I am now close friends with Midshipman Manning and do not hold the wound against him in the slightest. I was out of line, and he was simply doing his duty as an officer."

"Members?" Judge Griffith asked.

One of them stood up, "Midshipman Winters, do you believe Midshipman Manning to be engaged in espionage?"

"Objection!" Silver said.

"He is a character witness, your honor," Schmidt stated.

"Overruled, you are directed to answer the question."

"No," Richard said. "I do not believe that Midshipman Manning or any of his friends are conducting espionage, treason, or any form of spying."

"That's my only question," the member said, returning to his seat.

"Thank you, midshipman," the judge said. "Continue, Lieutenant Silver."

"I would like to present as evidence the Solar Fleet Regulations," Silver said. "Specifically, the paragraph that reads as follows: 'The Solar Fleet cannot enlist, commission, harbor, or assist a convicted criminal who has not fulfilled his/her sentence.'

"Commodore Andrus did not have the authority to accept these applications. I would like to stipulate that the Sky Marshal did not have the power to accept the applications of these midshipmen as they were convicted criminals, and they had not fulfilled their sentence."

"Sir," Schmidt said, standing.

"Continue," the judge said to Schmidt.

"I request a recess to address this stipulation."

"Granted," Judge Griffith said. "This court martial is recessed until 0900 hours tomorrow."

I got up, intending to snag Schmidt to talk with him, but as soon as recess was called, Schmidt shot up like a rocket, grabbed the Sky Marshal, and left the courtroom.

"Well, *he* left in a hurry," Marian noted.

"I wouldn't complain," Andrus said. "He's trying to save us."

We left, but before we could go to a restaurant, Jack Dalton intercepted us.

"Howdy," he said. Today his t-shirt read: "I'm a Fan of Kelven!"

"Hello," I returned.

"Our mutual friend wants to talk with you."

"Okay."

*Ardent or Sonnel?* I asked, opening a comm link with Mr. Dalton.

*Ardent.*

"Well," I said, turning to Richard and Commodore Andrus. "It appears I'll have to take a rain check for today's lunch. See you later."

They nodded, and we hopped into a small car that Dalton used. Before long, we were back in Mr. Dalton's office, and Ardent was there waiting for us. We exchanged greetings, and he started asking us about reactions we had when using the implants. I spent the afternoon and evening with them, before returning to my hotel room.

\*\*\*

"All rise for the military judge!" the bailiff called out.

The judge and the members entered, and we were all seated.

"I call this session to order," the judge said. "Lieutenant Silver, you have the floor. Use it wisely."

"I have no further witness to call, nor do I have any more evidence to present," Silver said.

"Does the defense have any witness they wish to call to the stand at this time?" the judge asked Schmidt.

"Yes," Schmidt said. "I would like to call Sky Marshal Bartholomew Kitt to the stand."

The Sky Marshal was in full dress uniform whites, the single golden sunburst of the Sky Marshal on his collars, his chest covered with many medals and awards. He even had a handgun strapped to his leg. The Sky Marshal settled into the chair as if it was his chair on the flagship, SFS *Sky*. He looked like he owned the universe, which, in some ways, he did. Captain Griffith swore him in and seemed grateful to turn his gaze back on Schmidt.

"Sky Marshal," Schmidt said. "Is the Solar Fleet currently on a war footing?"

"Yes," he said coolly. "We are currently at war with the Draconian Empire, and we are also at war with the UME."

"Sky Marshal, what powers do you gain in relation to Fleet regs during a declared war?" Schmidt asked.

"I gain the ability to change the regulations as I see fit, and I also gain the ability to ignore them, if I deem it necessary. I do not gain the power to override the UCMJ, but I can change regs."

"Did you deem it necessary to accept the application of Midshipman Manning and his friends?"

"Yes, I did," the Sky Marshal said. "I judged that they would be a significant asset to the Fleet, and I didn't want their lives to be wasted by allowing President O'Brien to kill them."

"Do you support the actions of Commodore Andrus?" Schmidt said.

I tensed, remembering Article 37. Schmidt had just called Silver on her bluff, but was it a bluff?

"Objection!" Lieutenant Silver jumped up out of her seat, almost knocking the chair over. "If the Sky Marshal answers that question, he will influence the decisions of the members. Article 37!"

The judge pondered for a while, and I knew our fates would probably be determined by this one decision made by the judge. Almost a full minute ticked by before he finally spoke. "What is your basis for this objection?" the judge asked. "Article 37 relates to unlawfully influencing the court. Is this not lawful?"

Silver responded, "I quote; 'No … commanding officer may … admonish the court … with respect to the findings … of the court. No (commanding officer) may attempt to influence by unlawful means … the actions of the court.'

"There was a case in the twenty-second century, United States Government vs. Lieutenant Packard. Lieutenant Packard's mother was a three-star admiral. The court sent a formal letter to Admiral Packard requesting that she 'not be present for the court martial of your son as your presence could be viewed as threatening to the members. We do not want to deal with any issues relating to Article 37 of the UCMJ.'

"There are many other cases which are similar to this one," Silver said. "I am transmitting the full list to the members."

"Excuse me, Lieutenant Silver, but all of these cases seem to involve relatives of the accused."

"They do, sir."

"The Sky Marshal is not a direct relative to any of the accused, is he?"

"He is not, sir. You would be setting a new precedent, but these previous cases point directly to such a decision."

"So you want me to decree that the Sky Marshal cannot act as a witness in any court-martial, because he is the Sky Marshal?"

"Yes, sir."

"What about four-star Admiral Cestari?"

"No, sir. The same would not apply to her."

"So you want me to decree that the Sky Marshal is disqualified from testifying in any court martials?"

"Yes, sir. Because of his unique position and influence, allowing him to testify would risk the impartiality of the jury and would threaten the independence and integrity of military judicial proceedings."

"Then your objection is overruled. The Sky Marshal is allowed to testify in court-martial cases. His actions so far do not constitute unlawfully influencing the court."

Silver stared at the judge with her mouth open for a moment before her aide pulled her down into her seat.

"You are directed to answer the question," the judge said.

"Objection!" Silver jumped up again. "Irrelevant."

"Remain in your seat Lieutenant JG Silver! I have already overruled you once. Please remain in your seat."

Silver returned to her seat.

"Continue," the judge said.

"I did and do support the actions of Commodore Andrus," the Sky Marshal said.

"No further questions," Schmidt said.

Silver stood up more slowly. She rubbed her temples for a second. "I have no questions for this witness."

"I would now like to present evidence," Schmidt said. "Everyone here knows Admiral Cestari. Her mother's, mother's maiden name was Gauge. I spent quite some time confirming the genealogy, and it appears that Midshipman Gauge and Admiral

Cestari are closely enough related for a DNA test to conclusively confirm their relationship. I had the DNA test run by Dalton Space Industries."

Schmidt handed a pad to each of the members. "As you can see, DSI has confirmed the midshipman to be a second cousin of the admiral within one degree of removal. Thus, Gauge could not, in fact, be a spy, since DSF has demonstrated that she is the one and only Annabeth Gauge."

"Excuse me," Commodore Young said. "How can you rule out spying?"

"The members are not permitted to ask questions at this time," Silver said.

"I would like to answer the question, sir," Schmidt said.

"Please proceed," the judge said.

"Military personnel not in disguise nor acting under false pretenses are specifically excluded from the definition of spying under the UCMJ. Therefore, since DNA evidence has positively confirmed that Midshipman Gauge is who she claims to be, it is impossible for her to be a spy."

"Thank you," Commodore Young said.

Schmidt continued, "If you will continue to scroll down, I have listed the genealogies of the other three midshipmen in question and have done DNA tests to prove that they also are who they say they are.

"With that, the defense rests."

I was shocked at how short Schmidt's case had been. He had seemed so worried, and yet he had used only about a quarter of the time that Silver had used. I hoped the courts' ruling would vindicate his judgment.

"Commander Schmidt, will the accused be availing themselves of pre- or post- Gadsden trial procedure?"

"Post-Gadsden, your honor."

"Understood. Commodore Andrus, Captain Belnap, Midshipmen Manning, Kade, Gauge, Spaceman Recruit Taggart, and Cadet Thomas, you have the right to make a statement. Included in your right to make a statement is the right to testify under oath, or to make an unsworn statement, or to remain silent. If you testify under oath, you may be cross-examined by the trial counsel or questioned by me or the members. However, if you make an unsworn statement, you may not be cross-examined or questioned by me or the members. You can have your unsworn statement presented orally or in writing, personally or through your counsel. If you choose, you may also use a combination of these methods. If you decide to remain silent, that cannot be held against you in any way. Do you understand your rights?"

"Yes," Andrus said.

"Very well," Judge Griffith said. "What do you choose?"

"We wish to make sworn statements, orally, and in person."

"Very well."

We each made a sworn statement, starting with me and ending with Commodore Andrus. We were asked a handful of questions, but there were no surprises during these statements. That is, until Annabeth gave hers. Schmidt had discussed having Annabeth make an unsworn statement, as Silver obviously wanted to question her. Although choosing to remain silent technically couldn't be held against Annabeth, Schmidt decided that, with a stacked court, it would be too risky to rely on that technicality.

"Midshipman Gauge, did you feel that you were asked to join the Fleet under duress?"

Annabeth smiled at her. "I had two choices," she said. "One was to wait until the President of the United States killed me and the other was to join the Fleet. If you believe that means I joined under duress, it is not Commodore Andrus' fault. He offered me an escape from death, and I jumped at it."

"Is it true that you do not intend to stay in the Fleet?"

"No," Annabeth said. "That is not true. However, I will not be attending the Academy. I just received my orders this morning. As soon as this trial is over, I will go to Harvard to earn a law degree, and I will then join your own admirable profession. I've joined the JAG Corps."

Silver was surprised. She obviously hadn't known Annabeth's intentions. "Then you are staying in the Fleet?"

"Yes, I intend to stay in the Fleet. I wish to become a lawyer."

"No further questions," Silver said, sitting down.

I wondered just how Silver had known that Annabeth didn't want to stay in the Fleet, but, in the end, it seemed to have hurt her case more that it had helped.

Finally, we proceeded to the closing arguments.

"Does the trial-counsel have a closing statement to make?"

"Yes, your honor," Silver said, standing up and walking over to the members. "You have all heard the President of the United States say that he has the legal right to sentence these midshipmen to death. You have heard the testimony of the man who forged their applications, stating that he did indeed falsify information on their applications. You have also seen the forged applications, and, as such, know that these midshipmen should not have been given their commissions. All of the officers being tried should be found guilty of all charges and specifications."

"Does the defense have a closing statement?"

"Yes, sir." Schmidt now walked over, and took Silver's place in front of the members. "You have all heard the most important testimony: that of Sky Marshal Kitt. He believes that these officers are all innocent, and he supported their actions taken by these officers. You have also seen the DNA proof that these midshipmen are who they say they are. If President O'Brien was wrong about the accusation of spying, it seems likely that he is equally incorrect for accusing these midshipmen of espionage and treason. We cannot convict people without any evidence. Yes, their applications contained incorrect information, but they were operating under a tight deadline imposed by the President. Can you honestly fault them for their actions? What would you have done differently? I ask that you find these officers not guilty of all charges and specifications."

Schmidt sat down.

The judge turned to the members, "How long do you need to deliberate on your decision?"

The ranking member stood. "We should be finished within an hour. I suggest a temporary recess."

"Granted," the judge said. "This court is recessed for one hour."

"Well, what do you think?" I asked Schmidt.

"I'm not sure. We presented a very strong case, but we still have to remember that half of the members are in O'Brien's pocket. It will be very close either way."

Schmidt obviously didn't want to talk, and the rest of us were too nervous to talk. So, we sat in silence, waiting for the verdict.

\*\*\*

"This court is called to order. Admiral Geary, you have the floor."

Admiral Geary stood. "We are by no means unanimous, but with a vote of five to seven, we have reached a final verdict."

"Please announce your verdict."

"All of the accused have been found to be innocent of all charges and specifications."

The judge nodded. "The court is adjourned."

He stood up and left.

"We did it!" Schmidt said, showing evident relief.

"Thanks," Annabeth said, hugging Commander Schmidt.

"Annabeth," I said.

"Oh, um, sorry," Annabeth said as she let go of Schmidt.

"It's okay," Schmidt said, smiling.

"I think Annabeth expressed our feelings best," I said. "But we are all thankful. You're a formidable JAG."

"Thanks."

I invited Schmidt, Andrus, Belnap, and the Sky Marshal to all come with us to the Spaceman's Asteroid. We chatted aimlessly for hours over lunch. The Sky Marshal was only able to stay for one round before he left for the SFS *Olympus*.

He motioned me to walk with him out of the bar.

"Well, Almek," he said. "You have survived the court martial, but will you survive the wrath of President O'Brien? I confronted him in private about the assassins. He wouldn't admit anything, but he knows we've been alerted. Keep your eyes and ears open for trouble. You may find a vibro in your back, if you're not meticulously careful."

"I'll be careful, sir."

"Good. You know my code. If you ever need help, just code for me. And, Almek, good luck at Boot Camp."

"Thank you, sir," I said saluting. He saluted back, and we parted ways. I headed back to the bar, while he proceeded to his ship.

After a couple more rounds of drinks, we all returned to our hotels, carefully guarded by Lieutenant McFarland and his men.

# Part 3
# Boot Camp

# Chapter 12
## Boarding the SFS *Midshipman*

The day after the court martial was over, Richard introduced us to Triad, an amazing zero g sport. The following week passed like a dream, as we spent most of our time either playing Triad or playing Richard's favorite computer game, Space Tactics.

But then the horrible day finally arrived. It was time to say good-bye. The SFS *Midshipman* wouldn't depart until 0900, because it had to wait for three other ships from earth to rendezvous with her. Even though we had stayed up late at the bar, we still got up early, so that we could play one last round of triad. Then the moment came. My squad was gathered at the tube that connected the SFS *Midshipman* to Dalton Spaceways.

"You are the best squad I will ever have. The time may come when I have to call on all of you for support, and I trust I will always be able to count on each of you. No other squad in London Proper could have done what we did to get out of London and reach Dalton Spaceways. No other group of teens could have done that. I know that each of you will serve the Solar Military with distinction. Good luck to all of you, and take my blessing also, for what it is worth. Live well, and if you are required to, die with honor."

"We will," Marian said. "Semper Fi!"

"I would love to go with you, Almek, but my dreams call me," Kai said.

Annabeth looked me in the eye, "Can I talk to you in private?" she asked.

"An officer in the SF is not allowed to deny that request," I said.

We walked away from the others as they were all exchanging their last words.

"Almek," she said. "You cannot forget the old squad, and I'm not referring to us, but to all of those who have died. You may be the only midshipman at the Academy who has had soldiers die under his command. Do not *ever* forget the price that comes with war, even if sometimes you have to accept that price, as we did when we escaped from London Proper."

"I know Annabeth," I said. "Losses are not acceptable, even if sometimes they must be accepted."

"Exactly," she said. She reached up, and placed her hand on my cheek. "Almek, also remember that you need time to have fun. Don't give up triad."

I smiled. "Don't worry, I won't."

She smiled knowingly. "There may be a day that you will want to give it up."

"I hope not."

She seemed to be staring deep into my soul. Then she glanced at the others and broke the silence. "If you ever get into any legal trouble, call on me, Fleet JAG Annabeth Gauge."

"I hope I don't ever need to have a JAG defend me again, but you'd be my first choice," I said

She stood up straighter and gave me a light kiss on my cheek.

We walked back to the others. I gave each of them a hug. Then we all stepped back. Richard, Jenny, Kris, and I stepped back in the direction of the tube, while Annabeth, Marian, and Kai stepped back towards the station's main passageway. Then we all stood at rigid attention and saluted each other.

"All midshipmen and spacemen recruits assigned to SFS *Midshipman* report immediately to the boarding hatch."

We broke our salutes, each of us did an about-face, and we walked coolly towards the tube. None of us looked back, we walked willingly and proudly into our new future in the Solar Military.

We were among the last sailors to board, and, as a result, we weren't able to get seats together. I grabbed a seat near the front. I chose that seat because the girl sitting in the seat closest to the bulkhead was very good looking. She looked tall even sitting down.

She had a thin build. Her long brown hair hung halfway down her back, and her vibrant green eyes sparkled with an inner light.

I sat down next to her, and she looked up at me.

"Hi," I said.

"Hello," was the only response she gave before her eyes darted back to the pad in her hands.

Though I could have enjoyed watching her, I pulled out my computer, opened the mod creator for Space Tactics and started working on one of my ship designs.

"All personnel, this is Captain Sims. Buckle up. We will be arriving at Boot Camp in two short hours."

I worked on changing the positions of the weapons to allow the greatest attack and defense flexibility. After about ten minutes, I saw the girl start to glance over at my pad. Finally, she broke the silence.

"What are you working on?"

"Designing a starship."

"For what?"

"Space Tactics."

"That's a Space Tactics ship?" she asked.

"Do you play Space Tactics?" I asked.

"Yeah," she said. "Everyone who wants to join the Fleet does. It's common knowledge that Space Tactics is heavily based on Academy training software, but what program are you using? I just played the standard Space Tactics. I didn't know you could customize stuff for it."

"Its a patch one of my friends created," I replied.

"Interesting. How long have you been playing Space Tactics?" she asked.

"A couple of weeks."

"A couple of weeks! I've been playing it for years. Where have you been?"

"It's a very long story," I replied.

"In other words, you just don't want to tell me?"

"Not until I at least know your name. I'm Almek Manning."

"Jade Robins."

"Nice to meet you, Jade."

"You, too, Almek."

"So where are you from?" I asked her.

"Kansas."

"Kansas? How did you end up in space?"

"That's how. I didn't want to stay in Kansas forever, and the Fleet was willing to take me into space. So, I jumped at the opportunity. What about you?"

"I was born in New York, but I spent most of my time in space."

I saw her beautiful green eyes light up with astonishment. "Do you mean Manning as in Andrew Manning, Captain of the UES *Mayflower*?"

"Yes," I said. "Andrew Manning was my father."

"Holy cow! I thought Manning's son was fighting for the Brits in the UME?"

"No, I'm right here."

Her green eyes darkened. "Are you a spy?"

"No!" I said.

"How in the world were you let into the Solar Fleet? Surely, they think you could be a spy?"

"The Solar Fleet trusts me, Jade. I was sponsored by the Sky Marshal."

"Right. And I was sponsored by a Draconian."

Jade turned her back to me and looked at her pad again. I struggled for words. Then I glanced across the aisle. Jenny was sitting there staring at me.

*Leave it for now,* she told me.

*I will,* I nodded back.

Why did Jade think I was a spy? She didn't even want to hear my story. She just jumped directly to conclusions. It didn't seem logical to me. About ten minutes later, Jade finally turned back to me. She had a huge grin on her face, and her green eyes were sparkling with laughter.

"You are so gullible, Almek," she laughed at me.

"Huh?" was the only reply I could think of.

Jade started laughing again, and it was a beautiful laugh. "You're so thick, maybe you are a Brit spy."

"Am not!"

"I know that," she said. "It was a joke! Though I do want to know why you backed down."

"I was advised by a good friend to drop it."

"Who? No one said a thing to you."

"Jenny over there," I said nodding at her. "Sent me an e-mail."

"A girlfriend?" she asked.

"Jenny?" I laughed.

"What, Almek?" she called across the aisle.

"I'm not talking *to* you, just *about* you," I said, turning to her.

"Thanks for letting me know," she said sarcastically. "What are you talking about behind my back?"

"Jade, here," I said, waving my hand at her, "just asked if you were my girlfriend."

We both shared a laugh at that.

"Jade," Jenny said. "Don't worry, Almek's available."

Jade didn't even blush, but her green eyes still sparkled with laughter. "I was not asking for my own benefit, simply to create small talk."

"Uh-huh?" Jenny said, raising her eyebrows.

"Well, are you up for a game of Space Tactics?" I asked Jade.

"Sure."

I messaged Richard and Kris. We soon had Jade, Jenny, Richard, Kris, and I all on a small game of Space Tactics.

\*\*\*

"You guys are good," she said, taking her headphones off, and shutting down her computer. "Really good for only having played for a couple of weeks."

"Thanks," I said.

We talked about Boot Camp for a while, then the captain spoke over the ship intercom.

"This is Captain Sims speaking. We are approaching Boot Camp. Prepare to disembark. Please turn to the screens on the chairs in front of you, and watch the introductory video."

I looked up at the chair, and I saw a small screen showing pictures of barracks, forests, and other buildings.

"Welcome to Boot Camp," a female voice said. "This station has been turned into one hundred square miles of forests, lakes, cliffs, and mountains. The best military strategists, and psychologists all agree that the best place to train soldiers is in the outdoors, so the Fleet has designed this station with optimizing your training as the sole objective.

"This camp uses techniques that the earth militaries have used for centuries. However, there is one way in which this training camp is unlike any other. At Boot Camp, both enlisted spacemen recruits and midshipmen train together. Four hundred will be assigned to each camp, divided into four teams of one hundred each. These teams will learn together, exercise together, and compete in all activities together. The team who does the best in all activities by the end of the four-week training period will receive full liberty privileges at the Academy. Along with that you will receive an honors graduate award that may be worn on your uniform.

"Your training will cover many subjects. You'll have classes covering rank recognition, first aid, and flight and battle simulations. You will also be trained in weapons, including both laser and ballistic. The weeks you spend here will probably be the most challenging you have ever experienced.

"Your final exam will be an intricate battle stations drill that will involve all of the recruits and midshipmen left at Boot Camp. If you make it through, you will either graduate as a spaceman in the Fleet or continue at the Academy as a midshipman. Not all midshipmen will graduate as such, but may be given the option of leaving, becoming a spaceman, or becoming a chief petty officer.

"You will be fully briefed by your RDC, recruit division commander, upon arrival. All electronics are to be left on your seat. They will be returned to you on your outbound voyage if you pass, or on an earth-bound voyage if you fail. Best wishes in your service to the everlasting glory of the Solar Fleet!"

The vid ended, and I turned to face Jenny.

*I'm glad that the Sky Marshal put us in the same company, but did he leverage us into the same recruit division?*

Before Jenny had a chance to respond, we were interrupted by a petty officer, who was standing at the front of the aisle.

"I am instructor Petty Officer Samuel Rogers. I will be the recruit division commander for Division Alpha. All whose names I read, stand up and exit the *Midshipman* behind me. Anyone caught with electronics will be awarded their first demerit. Ten demerits, and you will pack your bags and return to Dalton Spaceways."

He then began to read. He called out Jennifer Kade, and then a little later Almek Manning, then Kristine Taggart, and finally Richard Winters. Unfortunately, he didn't call Jade Robins. We followed the Petty Officer out.

"So he did swing it for us," I whispered to Richard and Jenny.

"That he did," Richard said. "Though it would have been interesting seeing you two pitted against each other."

"Interesting isn't the right word for it," Jenny said.

I smiled to myself. "You see, Richard, the Sky Marshal understands our chemistry. We work together as squad-builders. We umm ... what's the civilian term ... we network. If we hadn't been on the same side, we would have built our own squad, and it could have messed up the training techniques."

"Interesting," Richard said, nodding. "The Sky Marshal seems to really trust you."

"You will probably still build your own squad," Kris said.

I nodded thoughtfully, "Probably."

The scenery was amazing. When we exited the ship, we walked through a large hangar that held the *Midshipman* and her sister ships, which had brought up other Solar Fleet midshipmen and spacemen recruits. The moment we exited through a side door of the hangar, we were in a massive grassland. Richard turned around, and gasped. This caused the rest of us to turn around. We were staring at a door that opened into a hangar, but all around the door was blue sky, with grasslands beyond.

"Holo technology," he gasped. "They were lying to me. This is so much more advanced than what I was told we had at R&D. I knew it! The Sky Marshal will hear about this."

"That's the third time you've spoken of the Sky Marshal personally," Rogers observed.

"Yes," I said. "We are the three sailors," I pointed to Jenny and Kris, "who were on trial for treason, espionage, and spying, and Richard and the Sky Marshal were witnesses in our trial."

"Ah, interesting. I am surprised I was not briefed about you. That is why you are in uniform? You've been sworn in?"

"Yes, sir, the Sky Marshal swore us in," Jenny said.

"And the four of you know each other well?"

"Yes," I said. "Jenny, Kris, and I have saved each others lives many times. We have fought together for several years, while Richard has tried to kill us once and helped save us once."

"I really should have been briefed on you guys," the Petty Officer complained. "You lot are going to make things complicated. What do you mean you've fought together?"

"I led a squad in London Proper."

Petty Officer Rogers sighed heavily. "Do you follow orders well?"

Jenny and Richard both started laughing.

"Petty Officer Rogers," Jenny said. "If there's one thing Almek hates doing, it's taking orders."

Rogers groaned. "Then you're not going to be very happy. You were not selected as recruit commander."

"I'm not surprised," I said.

"What?" Rogers said.

"The Sky Marshal wouldn't have made it that easy. He wants me to learn. He knows my greatest flaw is not obeying orders."

We had left the grassland behind and entered a forest, before we started hearing complaints.

"Petty Officer," a girl whined. "How much farther do we have to walk?"

"Just two miles to go. If you recruits want to pick up the pace, we could get there a lot sooner. The more you complain, the harder it will be for all of you," Rogers said, raising his voice. "Since the recruit complained, we'll pick up the pace but add a one-mile detour to keep us on schedule."

I turned to Jenny. "Does this remind you of the march we made when Drake and Duke chased us to the outskirts of London Proper?"

Jenny smiled. "It does. That was when we were working with Kathy's squad."

The last two words brought back many memories. I wondered if Kathy and her squad were okay. Many of them had risked their lives to help us out of London Proper. I remembered my promise to go back, and I committed to myself that creating an opportunity to rescue them would be a top priority.

Richard jumped into the conversation by asking a question.

"Almek, Jenny, I have put off asking this question for quite awhile, but I just have to know. What happened to London?"

Jenny and I sighed in unison.

"Well," Jenny began. "I guess we'll have to start with the Draconian blockade for London's history to make sense. In response to the blockade, the United Earth government sent their whole small and rather puny fleet to fight the Draconians. The fleet consisted of US, British, and Australian warships. Half way there, the Australians broke rank and headed back to earth. The US Ships opened fire on them in a panic. After the ensuing battle, the shattered fleet, held together by the Sky Marshal, proceeded to reconnoiter the Draconian guard. That's how we learned most of what we know about them. Then the Sky Marshal turned the fleet around and returned home. None of these ships had K-drives and, when they returned to earth, they found the Civil War underway, with much stronger spaceships fighting in both earth and lunar orbit.

"During the war, London was heavily bombed with kinetic rounds from orbit, and its infrastructure was shattered. Those who survived, fled the city, leaving Greater London a deserted ruin. British sailors in the Sky Marshal's fleet tried to find work after the cease-fire, but most of those men and women failed to find a place in the struggling civilian economy. So, they moved to London and formed gangs that were originally called cadres. These cadres consisted of enlisted personnel from each of the five ships that survived the trip to the blockade: the *Arrow*, the *Swift*, the *Wellington*, the *Tiras*, and the *Devoted*.

"Those were the names of the first five cadres. These cadres lived and worked together for the first year. Then things turned bad. Food was scarce, and the weather was horrible. The cadres dropped the names of their ships and adopted the names of their leaders. The cadres also splintered into smaller groups, typically no larger than fifteen and started to refer to themselves as squads.

"It wasn't until the second year, that cooperation broke down due to scarce resources and raiding began. Many non-military spouses fled with younger children, while full-scale battles erupted between the remaining adults desperate to provide for teenage children who chose to stay with them. The initial battles were brutal, leaving most of the Navy parents as casualties, while their teenage children inherited control of the streets.

"The UME had already shown they had higher priorities than re-integrating vets into civilian life and decided to quarantine them, by building a fence around London and effectively turning it into a prison camp. And that, in a nutshell, is how the home we knew as London Proper came into being."

"You may call it a nutshell, but it's more than I've ever been able to learn. How do you know all of these details, Jenny?" Richard asked.

I felt a massive wave of emotion from Jenny. It was a strange feeling, and I jerked and looked over at her. *Why did he have to ask that question, Almek?* She asked via implant.

*I can answer if you prefer,* I offered.

*It's OK. I'll answer.*

"Richard," Jenny said. "My father served on the *Tiras*. My mother brought me to live with Father and the *Tiras* Cadre, at the beginning, when London's prospects still looked hopeful. When the battles started, I was ten. My father taught me how to use a vibroblade. Then one of the teenage squads, led by a very young petty officer, Duke Meade, attacked the *Tiras* cadre. They surprised our cadre, and the cadre was killed down to the last man, except for me. I lay almost dead next to the body of my father when I was picked up by another squad. One of the teenage squads. They healed me. I spent a year in that squad. Then I deserted one squad after another, trying desperately to find a squad I could accept as family. Finally, I ran into Almek and his dog, Saph. And Almek succeeded at forming a family that I could fit into. And before you have to puzzle over why I'm loyal to Almek, now you know."

I was blushing and looking down at my feet, while Jenny continued.

"Though I'm a year older than Almek, I often think of him as an older brother, the sibling I never had."

I finally butted in. "To be fair, Jenny is the one who kept me alive, especially in the early days of my squad. I would have been killed out of ignorance, if she hadn't trained me up. So, in truth, it's me who thinks of the other as an older sibling."

*You'll lose the one-upmanship game in the end,* Jenny laughed at me.

Richard glanced sharply at Jenny, with a rather puzzled look and shook his head.

"Okay, we get it," Rogers laughed. "You both owe each other your lives, and you both feel as if you're family." His tone suggested joviality, but I could sense that he understood the pain of Jenny's past.

Since we had already plunged into personal details, Richard had to get one more question off his chest, "Jenny, was your mother one of the ones who left?"

Jenny sighed heavily. "I don't know. We passed the days leading up to the battle with Duke's squad in a confused blur. I don't know if my mom died in that battle, or if she is still living in Britain somewhere. Someday I will try to find her, but I'm not ready yet."

Richard was silent for quite some time. "I'll never understand, will I?" he asked.

"No," I said. "It would be hard to fully understand, without moving to London Proper."

"Manning," Rogers said. "Since Jenny has told her history, how did *you* end up on the streets of London Proper?"

I smiled, and told my story, and Richard, in turn, told how he became involved in technology after his dad was killed in an explosion on a commercial ship when it was upgraded to K-drive propulsion.

At the end of our story swap, Rogers muttered, mostly to himself, "You three are going to make these next four weeks very interesting."

# Chapter 13
## Day One

The remainder of the hike to Boot Camp was fairly uneventful, and the camp itself was rather dull looking. There were two clusters of four barracks, each at one end of the camp. The gym was in between those two clusters, and a track and a small library were next to the gym. Beyond that was what Rogers called the "games pavilion," though I doubted it had very good games compared to Space Tactics and Triad. Then, past the games pavilion was the mess hall, and, below the mess hall was the officers' quarters and the office. The only thing at the camp that was impressive was the massive building north of the library. This building towered above the other buildings and was three or four times larger than all the other buildings combined. We would later find out that this building housed the holochamber.

Petty Officer Rogers took Division Alpha to the two barracks closest to the holochamber.

"The barracks on the right is the boys' barracks, the barracks on the left is the girls' barracks. However, before you split up, now is your last chance to get rid of all electronics. I noticed a lot of you still have watches. Those have to go also, unless you have mechanical watches."

A couple of kids deposited the electronics they had snuck off the spaceship. Then Rogers turned back to the group. "Remember, those of you who still have electronics can turn them in now for one demerit. Otherwise, you'll get two when we do a search of the barracks and your persons tomorrow."

A few more kids gave up their electronics and identified themselves. Rogers marked them down on a paper notepad. "Okay, now comes the moment you've all been waiting for. Your team leader is Midshipman Isaac Jones! Midshipman Jones, step forward."

The kid stepped forward. He didn't look like much of a leader, but I needed to get used to being commanded by inferiors sooner or later.

*Watch it, Almek,* Jenny said.

*Did you hear that?* I asked.

*Yes, your thoughts are leaking through again,* she said. *You need to be more careful.*

*Well, Jen, it seems that the two us can open a comm link between us without realizing it.*

*True.*

"Cadets Manning and Kade, face front!" Rogers spat.

I jumped to attention, and so did Jenny.

"As I was saying, there will also be a leader in the girls barracks. This leader has no authority outside of the barracks or the mess hall. She is simply there to maintain order when away from the recruit commander. This leader is the very one not paying attention. Midshipman Jennifer Kade, step forward."

She did, and despite the chewing out she had just received, she stared straight into the eyes of Petty Officer Rogers.

"I accept the responsibility."

*You get to be commander, but not me?* I asked incredulously.

*Shut up! We'll have to figure this out later, ending link.*

"Okay," Rogers said. "You guys have twenty minutes to settle in. Dinner starts at precisely 1900, and if you're not there at 1900, you'll find the doors closed and locked. You'll be out of luck until 0700. One last thing, you will all find a navy blue jumpsuit with your name on the table in your bunkhouse. You are to wear that to dinner. All except for the three already sworn in as midshipmen and the spaceman."

Rogers pivoted and headed towards the officers' quarters at a brisk jog.

"What did you two think of that?" I asked Jenny when Rogers was gone.

"He is singling us out," Jenny said. "But I don't know why. We haven't done anything yet."

We stood in silence for a while, then Richard looked up, "We'd better get a move on it, before the good bunks are all snagged."

We nodded to Jenny and Kris and went to our bunkhouse. We got in and found only one bunk left, right by the door. We found our jumpsuits and our gear that someone had brought down from the ship, placed them on our bunks, and hurried off to the mess hall.

*Jenny, you done yet?* I asked her.

*No, I'll be a little late.*

I was about to say something to Richard, but I noticed he had stopped a couple of paces behind me and looked a little worried.

"Richard?" I asked.

He shook his head. "Sorry," he ran to catch up.

"What happened?"

"Nothing," he said, shaking his head again.

I nodded and walked to the mess hall. We weren't the first ones there. I heard someone playing a guitar and singing one of my favorite songs:

*We've wandered from land to land,*
*We've traveled throughout the earth,*
*And we'll never conquer our wanderlust,*
*Nor find that it had a birth.*

*We've traveled to moon and asteroid,*
*We've traveled throughout our space,*
*But no matter how far we've wandered,*
*We'll never finish the race.*

*The mysteries of the heavens*

*Bewitch like the sirens' call,*
*And we'll never borrow Circe's wax*
*To stop up our ears at all.*

*We've seen the Draconian border,*
*They've marked out the edge of our sphere,*
*But we'll always long to extend the song*
*And beyond our horizons to peer.*

*We hear the sirens calling,*
*To fly past the furthest star,*
*And we'll never conquer our wanderlust,*
*Even after we've flown that far.*

*We'll jet beyond the edge of our sphere,*
*The sirens' call is too strong,*
*But we'll always nurse a home in our heart,*
*For the planet we've loved so long.*

I had walked in part way through the song and was standing at the door.

"Well played," I said.

The midshipman playing an acoustic guitar looked up at me. "I … I didn't realize anyone else had arrived."

"It's okay, you play great, and your singing isn't half bad. That happens to be one of my favorite Rhysling songs"

"Interesting, what's your …" his eyes drifted to my name tag. "Manning? As in Andrew Manning?"

"No, Almek Manning," I said, smiling.

"Oh."

"Andrew was my father."

The midshipman laughed. "Sorry, Almek. I'm Bronski, Zack Bronski, but I prefer Bronski."

"And I'm Richard Winters," Richard said, sticking his hand out. They shook hands.

"Okay, Bronski. How long have you been playing the guitar?" I sat on the bench opposite him.

"Since I was eight. I love the guitar."

"What made you want to join the Fleet then?"

"I've wanted to space longer than I've wanted to play the guitar."

"Okay, well why don't you strike up another tune, while we wait for dinner."

He played a couple more songs before the other sailors started arriving. Once the mess hall was starting to get filled with the sounds of people chatting, Bronski pressed a button to retract his guitar, so he could fold it into a rod and sling it across his back.

"That's convenient," I said.

"Yup, I figure that way I can bring it on route marches. I have another guitar that I prefer, but I can play this one just as well, and it's allowed at camp…"

I nodded, and then we all stood up at a shout from an ensign.

"Attention on deck!"

I looked over at the entrance and saw a captain enter.

"I am Captain William Drake, the Commandant of Boot Camp," he said, as he took his place at the head of the officers' table. "You have all had to pass a test to get in here. The Fleet is picky about its sailors, and the Fleet wants only the best from its officers. This camp will not be easy. We usually lose twenty to fifty people in the first week. You are still young and may not be used to the harshness of war and military life. However, you are all qualified to join the Fleet. All except four of you, who have already been sworn into the Fleet. Richard Winters, Jennifer Kade, Kristine Taggart, and Almek Manning come up here with me."

Richard and I stood up and walked forward. Jenny and Kris also got up from their table. We all formed a line on the right of the Commandant.

"These three," he said, pointing to Jenny, Kris, and me, were sworn in by the Sky Marshal, because they were taking part in a military courts martial, but that is a topic for later discussion. I will have Midshipman Almek Manning lead you in the oath, and, in case any of you were wondering, he *is* the son of Andrew Manning. All of you in the midshipman program, stand and recite the oath."

The other midshipmen were going to hate me because of this, but I led the oath with pride, for I was part of the Fleet, and it is an honor to swear others into the Fleet. However, while I was reciting the oath, I saw my recruit commander, Midshipman Jones, glaring at me. When I was done, the Commandant spoke again.

"Now have a seat, midshipmen. All who are in the spaceman program, stand and recite the oath. Please follow Spaceman Recruit Kristine Taggart in the oath of enlistment.

"You are all sailors now and members of the Solar Fleet. I would like to point out that your oath is not a free pass. You have to work hard to remain a sailor in the Fleet. Welcome! And, dig in! All sailors line up at the buffet, ladies first."

Jenny headed over to the buffet.

"Jennifer Kade," the Commandant said. "I would like you and Almek Manning to sit at the officers' table tonight. I have some questions for you."

"Yes, sir," Jenny said.

"As the Commandant wishes," I said.

After I had gotten my food, which most of the sailors were already grumbling about, I headed over to the Commandant's table. I admit the food wasn't as good as the food I had eaten on Dalton Spaceways, but I figured it was still much better than the food I had eaten in London Proper.

The Commandant turned to me. "Is it true that you lived in the streets of London?"

"Yes, sir."

"My wife, my ex-wife lives in New Capitol, and, last I heard from her, our son had run away. We believe that he ended up in London Proper. Did you meet anyone by the name of …"

I grimaced and interrupted him. "Ethan Drake?"

"Yes, you met him?"

"You could say that," I said, hesitating.

"Is he okay?" the Commandant asked worriedly.

I looked straight into the Commandant's eyes. "I killed him in battle, sir."

The Commandant gasped. "He's dead?"

"Yes, sir," I said. "We commanded rival squads, and he had tried to kill me ever since I was stranded in London Proper."

"Squad commander?"

"Yes, sir. He had his own command. I can't say he led well, but he gave my squad a run for our money."

"I see," he said, a distant look in his eyes

The Commandant stood up and left the mess hall, and there wasn't another word spoken at the officers' table. Jenny and I finished quickly, and we asked for permission to leave. Permission was granted, and we headed back to the bunkhouses in silence. Richard, Kris, and Bronski caught up to us by the library.

"What was that about?" Richard asked.

"You remember what I told you about squad leader Drake, right?" I asked him

"The guy who always wanted to kill you?"

"Yeah, I just learned that Drake is the Commandant's son."

"Didn't he get killed by your squad?" Richard asked.

"No."

"Well, that's good," Bronski said.

"No, he wasn't killed by my squad," I explained. "I killed him personally, with a vibroblade."

"Oh boy," Bronski said. "You are so screwed."

"Yeah, I know," I muttered. "And just in case it helps any, Midshipman Jones hates me."

"How do you know that?" Bronski asked.

"He was glaring at me while I was leading you guys in the oath."

Kris nodded. "You do seem to make all the right enemies: the President of the United States, the Commandant's son, and even your recruit commander."

We reached our barracks and said good-bye to Jenny and Kris as we entered the boys' bunkhouse. Bronski played a couple more Rhysling tunes. Then we hit the sack. It was only 2000, but we all knew that we had to get up for reveille at 0445, and we were no longer operating on the twenty-five hour day of Dalton Spaceways.

***

Richard, Bronski, and I were all roused by reveille at 0445, changed into our jumpsuits and marched to the flagpole. I had contacted Jenny, and she said she was in the process of getting her lazy sailors out of their comfortable bunks.

We got to the flagpole, and we met up with a handful of others, maybe twenty other recruits and five instructors. Four of the instructors were petty officers, Rogers among them, and the other was an ensign I had met at dinner, Ensign Merryweather.

"I expected to see you early," Petty Officer Rogers said. "But where is Midshipman Kade?"

"She is trying to get the rest of her barracks down here."

"Well," Rogers said, looking at his watch. "She still has six minutes."

The flags of the Presidential Council and the Solar Fleet had been retired last night, and the flagpoles stood tall and empty.

"Who does the flag raising?" I asked.

"You do," Rogers said. "Not today, but, starting tomorrow, the midshipmen will raise the flags."

I nodded, then turned back to look for Jenny.

*You've got five minutes.*

*Understood. I have most of them ready.*

I turned back to Richard, and his eyes looked vacant. I was beginning to wonder if he was getting sick.

Jenny had all of her girls out of the bunkhouse and marching down toward the flagpole with just a minute to spare. The ensign ordered the petty officers to go to the bunkhouses and rouse the remaining sailors. It took another ten minutes to get them all down to the flagpole.

"Good morning, sailors," Ensign Merryweather began. "I see that you all thought you could get your beauty sleep this morning. I know you lazy louts can get up at 0445 for reveille. I am going to make sure you do. From now, on you will be here at 0500 sharp, ready to start the day. We will have thirty minutes of warm up exercises, then we will eat. Sick call is at 0600 if you wish to see the doctor. At 0700, we will have our real physical training until first call to colors at 0755. After the colors, each division has their own program, and your RDC will lead you."

After that, Ensign Merryweather tore into us. He chewed us out for not showing up on the bounce. His lecture lasted until 0600. Then he told us we would be skipping breakfast. There was a collective groan from all the sailors, and we were instructed to split up and follow our RDC.

Rogers chewed us out while we marched down to the track. We ran around that track so many times I lost count. I know Jenny and I must have run at least twenty klicks, because that's about the distance we could run in one and a half hours back in London. At 0750, Rogers marched us to gym, and we spent the next three hours there. At that point, I could tell that most people were about ready to die from lack of food. I bet that none of them had done a workout like this before on an empty stomach. Jenny, Kris, and I did fairly well, but we had gotten out of shape in the two weeks since London Proper. By the time all of the sailors had been gathered in the mess hall, it was 1100, and we were all hungry. Jenny, Kris, and I had been used to getting one meal a day in London Proper. Since then, we had gotten used to three squares a day. We recited the oaths together before we ate, and then we sat down and dug into our food.

"That was the hardest day of my life," Richard said after his tenth bite of mashed potatoes. "Even mil food is starting to taste good."

I laughed. "Richard, you haven't even finished the first day."

"I don't want to think about it! Let me live in the moment, Almek. Let me just live in the moment."

I looked up at the head of the table. "Petty Officer Rogers, just what are we doing the second half of the day?"

"Well," he said putting his fork down. "I guess I might as well tell everyone now. Division Alpha! Listen up! Today starts your p-days or processing days. For the rest of the day, all of you will be having full physicals done. More than what you did back earth-side. The best part is the shots you will be getting. You will all be vaccinated for every disease under our star. Everything from the bubonic plague to Venusian flu. You will be out of action tomorrow and will not be required to get up for morning drills. You will even have three small meals served in your barracks. This is not a luxury, as you will be in extreme pain and occasionally delirious. But you will survive. You have my word on that."

The whole table fell silent, and I didn't feel too confident until a message flashed across my vision. *You will be fine,* it read. *The implant provides nanos that can combat any disease known to humanity and even quite a few not yet known to humanity. The nanos will fight the vaccines, keeping the pain minimal.*

The message was signed "Ardent."

I sighed with relief, and my tour of the doctor's office, which ended up being just the mess hall with white soundproof temporary barriers installed, was quick and easy. Richard and Bronski on the other hand, did not have a fun time. They kept fretting about what tomorrow would bring, saying how much they hated getting shots and getting sick. Most of the division was able to eat dinner that night, but about twenty or so remained in the barracks, already feeling miserable.

That night no one slept well, not even me, because of all my suffering companions.

# Chapter 14
## P-Days

The next morning, I felt a little sick, like I had caught a cold or a mild case of the flu. I sat up and looked around the barracks. I saw that most of the sailors were sleeping fitfully. There was only one other sailor who looked like he wasn't about to die, and that was Richard.

"Richard," I called out. "Are you okay?"

"Yeah," he said, looking up at me. "I was stuck over a hundred times with diseases from earth, the dead disease from Luna, and even the one from Mars, but I feel okay. I don't get it."

Suddenly, I had a thought. I turned my implant's scanners up and, sure enough, my scans showed an implant in Richard. He, however, didn't appear to know about it. I checked my comm log, and I saw that almost every time I contacted Jenny, my link had been leaking to Richard's implant. So, it seemed that he had been getting a faint echo of our conversations, which would explain his strange behavior for the past couple of days.

I opened a link to both Richard and Jenny. I saw Richard jump as the request to open a comm link appeared in front of his field of vision. He looked up at me, confused. Then I saw him move his mouth.

*Jen, Richard, can both of you hear me?*

*Yeah, of course I can, but why would Richard?* Jenny asked.

*I can hear you,* Richard said, once again looking at me. *I'm not going crazy, then, or is this a Venusian flu dream?*

*No dream,* Jenny said. *But why wouldn't Ardent have told us?*

*Guys,* Richard said. *You two have a lot of explaining to do, and we're not doing anything, because we're all supposed to be sick. I assume you two aren't very sick, either?*

We started out answering his last question, and we had soon told him all about our meetings with Mr. Dalton, Sonnel the Third, and Ardent. We went on to explain about the implants, and how we had been tasked as liaisons to the Solar Fleet by the Canids. We also explained that the Solar Fleet was about to get a massive infusion of technology, once the Canids were ready. It was only after our talk with Richard, that we tried to contact Ardent. His 'plant was disconnected from the main network, and we were rerouted to someone else.

*This is communications officer Beta Three Dron of the Zochtil,* a Canid said. *Your signal is coming from Canid implants, and I request you identify yourselves.*

*This is Midshipman Almek Manning, Canid liaison to the Solar Fleet. I wish to speak to your executive officer, Ardent.*

*Understood, patching you through.*

*This is Ardent.*

*Almek here.*

*Hey Almek, what's up?*

*Richard Winters.*

I could almost see the smile in Ardent's canine face. *So you have discovered the implant.*

*Yes, we have.*

*Good, the only reason he wasn't informed of the procedure was that we weren't sure if you would want him to know right away. Sonnel said to leave it in your hands. She wanted Richard to have a 'plant. So he does.*

*Sometimes I wish ... I'm not sure, but thanks anyway.*

*Ending link,* Ardent said.

The connection died, and Richard, Jenny and I talked about the strangeness of aliens. Then I received a link request from Kai.

*Kai,* I said, as I ended the link with Richard and Jenny.

*Howdy!* He said. *I just got my first free moment, and I wanted to ask how things are going over there.*

*Things are great!* I said. *We haven't done much of anything yet though. Everyone here is recovering from vaccinations.*

*I'm glad implants help with that.*

*How's flight school?* I asked him.

*Great! I've got three weeks of book learning before I get behind a SAP. After Shuttle All-Purpose, it normally takes two weeks to pass the quals, and then I'll move up to an Alleycat, a small, but highly effective, two-person fighter. After the two months it takes to finish Alleycat quals and the Space Tomcat quals, it'll be time for flight duty stations and being posted to a station or a carrier.*

*That sounds fast,* I said.

*It is,* Kai explained. *But Mr. Dalton has put DSF on a war footing, and the Space Force has started double-timing the training. However, they aren't going to put inexperienced pilots in the cockpit of a Tomcat, so I'll have to stay sharp to get up to that stage. Once I make it to the Tomcat, they won't waste time with pleasantries. They'll push me straight through and into the Force.*

*Cool,* I said. *Good luck.*

*You too. I have to run. Link my hellos to Jenny, Kris, and Richard for me.*

*Wait, you know about Richard?*

*Yeah, sure, Ardent told me last night.*

*Aliens,* I muttered.

*Ending link.*

I informed Jenny and Richard about Kai's status, and then the conversation took an interesting twist.

*So,* Jenny said. *What do you think of Jade?*

*What am I supposed to think about her?* I asked.

*It's obvious that you like her.* Jenny said.

*You do?* Richard asked.

*Richard, not now,* Jenny said, and I was sure that Jenny was shaking her head at him.

*Fine, I like her. You happy?*

*Maybe, maybe not. This isn't London Proper.*

*What is that supposed to mean?* I asked.

*You can't date someone under your command in the Fleet.*

*So?* I was still a little lost with where Jenny was going.

*You can't date an officer on your ship.*

Finally, it clicked. *Well, what if she wants to command a starship, too.*

*She doesn't,* Richard said. *I talked to her during the game. She wants to be a navigator.*

*There are lots of navigators in the Fleet,* I said.

*I know,* Jenny said. *Seeing how it went during the ride up here, she should be part of the squad.*

I felt the same way. *The squad is starting to grow again. Looks like we have two new members, Bronski and Jade.*

The day moved slowly at first, since we weren't allowed out of the barracks, but, after a while, we found a port for Space Tactics on the 'plant. We started up a game, and the day passed much quicker. My mind kept turning to the conversation about Jade, but I wouldn't be commanding a ship for years, so what would a relationship now hurt anything...

\*\*\*

The next day, we were all up at 0445 getting ready. Some of the sailors were taking showers, but I saw no point in a shower right before I was about to go exercise for an hour. The morning routine went as scheduled. Everyone was out of their bunks and down at the flagpole by 0500 as ordered by Ensign Merryweather. All except Division Bravo, which I assumed had just had their vaccinations.

After breakfast, our first stop was the gym, where a military haircut was given to each of us. All the enlisted men were shaved bald, while the midshipmen were allowed a little more hair, and the women's hair was cut off at the ears. Then we had more clothing issued to us. We were given a couple more jumpsuits, dress whites, service blues, and service khakis. We then were issued an identity orb, and an exchange card, which would allow us to make purchases at the camp's Fleet Exchange.

The testing started the following day. We were given many different types of aptitude tests, and the tests went on for the next three days. By the end of the last day, I was given a single sheet of paper that read as follows:

ALMEK MANNING
MIDSHIPMAN - NO HONORS
AGE - 18

COMMAND SKILLS - EXCELLENT
TAKING ORDERS - POOR
FLIGHT - POOR
NAVIGATING - OK
SMALL ARMS - EXCELLENT
WEAPONS - GOOD
COMMUNICATIONS - OK
ENGINEERING - OK
MEDICINE - N/A
LAW - GOOD
CHAPLAIN - N/A

RECOMMENDED    FIRST    ASSIGNMENT:    ACICO (ASSISTANT COMBAT INFORMATION CENTER OFFICER)

After I finished reading that piece of paper, Petty Officer Rogers started talking.

"Sailors! The scale on which things are graded starts from the bottom with N/A, meaning you have no interest in this subject whatsoever and training would be useless, then we have poor, OK, good, excellent, and one person out of the entire camp will receive superb in each subject, except for command skills. If you have a superb on your sheet then you are set. That is almost certainly the field you will go into, and our stats indicate you will excel in that field once properly trained. However, the aptitude tests are by no means perfect. Some of you may be great at something that was marked as poor. You will be assessed again after battle stations drill, and then you will be assessed again after the Academy, if you go there. At that point your first duty station will be assigned. So, don't worry, this is only the start of a long course of training before you are deployed."

After, everyone started comparing their sheets. Jenny, Jade, Richard, Bronski, and I walked away from the rest of the group, and headed to a small patch of trees that we had staked out during the few rest periods we were given.

"So how did you do in navigation?" I asked Jade.

Her vibrant green eyes were sparkling with joy, and her smile reflected that same joy. "I got superb."

*Superb,* Jenny said. *Not just any navigator, huh?*

*Ending link,* I hissed. I wasn't sure what to think anymore. We could really use her on our ship.

We had just reached our patch of trees when my least favorite person showed up, Isaac Jones.

"What do you want, sir?" I asked him, standing up.

"I want to see your paper."

"Request denied, sir." I couldn't understand what this kid's problem was, but he really hated me. He wanted to make sure I understood that he hated me.

"I outrank you. I'm giving you an order."

"With all due respect, I'm ignoring it, sir."

I was sitting down when Jones rammed into me with his shoulder and sent me flying. I hit a tree trunk hard. I gasped for breath and instinctively reached for my vibroblade. I mentally kicked myself, since midshipmen at Boot Camp aren't allowed to carry weapons. While I had wasted time reaching for a weapon that I no longer carried, Jones' fist collided with my jaw. Jenny pulled him off of me, and I was about to hit him a couple of times when one of Jones' friends, Daniel Lee, attacked Jenny. I laid into Jones, and we had a brawl underway. Richard, Bronski and a couple of Jones' other friends all joined in. It took five other sailors, and all four RDCs to break up the fight. Coming out of it, all of Jones' men looked worse off than mine, except for Richard who looked horrible. I didn't think he had ever been in a fight before. Bronski, on the other hand, appeared to me to be a natural at hand-to-hand combat. I made a mental note to ask him about that later on.

\*\*\*

Within minutes of Jones throwing the first punch, we were facing the Commandant of Boot Camp.

"I don't know what to do with you," the Commandant said. "I want to kick all of you out of my camp, and make you start over again next year."

My heart fell. If I didn't make it now, it might be too late. The war might start before I could graduate from the Academy.

"However, we have a war on. You all have exceptional aptitude scores, and the Fleet can't afford to have you kicked out yet, but cancelling your liberty privileges would definitely be appropriate."

Once again my heart fell. I had heard about liberty at Boot Camp, and it was supposed to be awesome. I might miss it because of an idiot commanding officer. Jones that is, not the Commandant.

"However, I think that would go beyond the punishment you deserve for a minor brawl. So, I have decided on a punishment that will fit the crime. You are fined your complete pay for the four weeks at Boot Camp. If you fight again outside of hand-to-hand combat class, you *will* lose your liberty privileges and you will regret it. Dismissed!"

We were led out of the Commandant's office, and Rogers pulled me aside.

"Look, Almek. You need to repair your relationship with Jones."

"He starts it every time."

"You sound like a little kid complaining about a bratty sister. Grow up, Almek! You are in the Solar Fleet. This isn't London Proper. You can't solve all of your problems by slipping a vibro between someone's ribs. Understood?"

"I didn't want to kill him," I said.

"There are cameras everywhere here. I saw you reach for your vibro. It's a good thing we haven't issued one to you, or we would have a dead midshipman on our hands, I think."

I looked down. When I had reached for my vibroblade I had been running on instinct and adrenaline. I honestly wasn't sure what I would have done next.

"What matters is that we don't have a dead midshipman on our hands, and it won't happen again. Outside of hand combat class, that is. During that class, I consider Jones fair game."

"But, remember, you must repair the relationship if you ever want to get your own command."

Rogers walked off, and I met up with Jenny, Bronski, and Richard who were on their way to the first aid tent.

"That was a close one back there," I said nodding to the Commandant's office.

"Too close," Richard said. "I think you need something to keep your mind off of Isaac Jones and to stay focused on your goal. I know you want to captain a ship, a starship, but you can't expect to do that with your level of mathematics. I assume you were fairly advanced when you went into London, but you obviously need to brush up. The Sky Marshal requested that, once we arrived at camp, I would start tutoring you and Jenny. The Academy doesn't teach any math courses below Trig, and if you have to start in Trig, you'll be significantly delayed."

I was staring at Richard opened mouthed. "I am so *stupid*!" I exclaimed. "How could I have forgotten about math?"

Richard smiled. "How about we get started?"

\*\*\*

The next week, we started classes. Petty Officer Rogers called it "back to school." I was taking lots of classes. My favorites were spacecraft and spaceship familiarization and ordnance and weapons, though my watch standing class was also really fun. I had also started enjoying my daily math tutoring sessions with Richard, who had, obviously, received a superb mark in engineering. He was set to be a chief engineer.

It was Friday night, and we were about to have our first day off. After exercising and breakfast on Saturday, we would have the rest of the day off.

Richard had left dinner early, and a couple minutes later Jenny and I went to the library to meet Richard.

"You know, I'm almost lookin' forward to school work," Jenny said, as we walked into the library.

"Yeah?" I said, raising an eyebrow.

"Yeah, I'm sick of all of this military stuff. It is nice to do something unrelated to the Fleet."

"Jenny, this is just like life in Britain," I said.

"No, it isn't," Jenny stated. "We … you were in complete command. The squad lived by your word. I guess I'm just not used to being one of the crowd. I was second in command of an awesome force. A force to be reckoned with. Now I am a middy in the Solar Fleet. A no one."

"Don't worry, we will eventually command more than we ever could have dreamed of back in London Proper."

"I don't know, I dreamed of a lot," Jenny said. "And with someone like Captain Drake writing our final report, you never know…"

"The two Brits are conspiring now?" a familiar voice scoffed.

I looked over to see Richard and Jade sitting at a table. Jade was smiling up at us.

"Richard?" I asked.

He smiled, "Jade asked me to tutor her, too. Do you think you can withstand the competition Almek?"

"Well, Jade, do you mind if the British traitors join you in math?"

"Not at all."

Jade smiled. "Come on, Richard was just starting me in on partial fraction decomposition."

"Sounds fun," I said.

"I'll stick to matrices." Jenny groaned and sat down next to Richard.

I pulled up a chair and sat down next to Jade.

"Now," Richard said, as he started explaining the complicated wonders of mathematics.

\*\*\*

That night, sleep didn't come easily. I kept thinking about my feelings for Jade. I really liked her, but … I already had the perfect XO, Jenny, my engineering officer, Richard, and now I could have the best navigator in Boot Camp. Then again, I most likely wouldn't even get any of them assigned to my ship. Not to mention the fact that I wouldn't be in the fleet for another four years and, even allowing for wartime promotion, I probably wouldn't make captain for at least another five. My thoughts kept running around in circles. I didn't fall asleep until long after lights out, when I finally decided that I wouldn't act on my feelings for Jade. Maybe at the academy I would find a better navigator or a girl I liked better. Either way, I wasn't going to do anything stupid yet. I would wait and see.

# Chapter 15
## Liberty

We woke up, exercised, and ate in giddy anticipation. There had been many rumors about what we would be doing today. Jenny, Richard, Bronski, and I all sat down at our usual table, and we were about to start eating when we heard a voice from behind us.

"Hey Almek." I turned, and it was Jade. "Do you mind if I have a friend join us?" Jade was motioning to another girl.

"Not at all."

"I'm Nicole Taylor, Recruit Commander of Bravo."

"Nice to meet you, ma'am."

"Don't ma'am me. We're all midshipmen here."

I smiled. "As you wish."

"I want to join your squad," Nicole said.

"If Jade vouches for you, you're in," I said. "I don't have a test. The only question I care about is if you fit with our team."

"From what I've observed and what Jade has told me, I think I will."

"Then, welcome aboard," Jenny said.

Captain Drake stood up from his seat at the officers' table, "Sailors, you have trained hard for two weeks, and you all deserve a break. You have spent fourteen days giving your best, and you are about to be asked to work a whole lot harder. And, for that reason, we are giving you one day off. Just one, and you will work the remaining fourteen days harder than you ever have in your lives. Whether you proceed to the Academy or directly into the Fleet will be based on the abilities you display during the next couple weeks of simulations.

"The holochamber is open. We have set up fifty chambers. You've each been allocated a time slot. You can combine times with your friends and do something together. The holochamber has been booked all day until dinner, when you will all be randomly paired with a member of the opposite gender. You will have dinner with your pair, and then there will be a dance in the holochamber. Reveille has been moved to 0700 tomorrow. Enjoy!"

I turned to my table. "Let's all do something together. Sound like a plan?"

"It depends," Jade said. "Just what would you guys want to do?"

I looked around. "Let's talk to Rogers, and see what the options are."

Before we could get up, Rogers was already at our table.

"Hey, as you guys are my favorite midshipmen I wanted to talk to you first. Here are your times, and here is the list of programs."

He passed out six sheets of paper, each with our time at the top and a list of programs below.

"Triad," I said. "Is holo Triad any good?"

"Feels just like the real thing," Rogers said.

"Sounds cool to me," I said.

"Yeah," Richard echoed. "I'm always up for Triad."

"I'm all over that," Bronski said.

Jade and Nicole agreed, and so it was decided.

We continued the Triad simulation for two hours, at which point our time ran out. We came out laughing and joking among ourselves. We still had a few hours before dinner, and we decided to go to the games pavilion. We pulled down a classic game that Nicole loved. She taught us the rules, and we spent the remaining time playing Agricola. Then Petty Officer Rogers came into the pavilion.

"Almek, I need to speak with you outside."

"I'm in charge of making matches for the dinner tonight. Do you want to pick a date? I know you've had you're eye on Jade."

I blushed up to my ears. "How about Nicole?"

"Chicken?" Rogers asked me.

"No," I said. "Look, Rogers, I want to command a starship. I want a navigator like Jade at the helm of that ship. I don't want to lose a good navigator, because we had a relationship that failed or we're involved in a relationship. At this point, I'm not willing to risk that."

"Sounds logical. Nicole it is then."

"What am I supposed to tell my friends about this meeting?" I asked Rogers.

He smiled. "Tell them I just wanted to change something on your aptitude sheet."

"What?"

"Make it up."

I turned and walked briskly into the games pavilion.

"What was that about?" Jade asked.

Figures she had to be the one to ask.

"Just something about my aptitude sheet."

"What?" Jade prodded.

"Yeah, what?" Nicole asked.

"Nothing important."

"Fine," Nicole said, letting the subject drop.

Before anyone else could speak up, Petty Officer McCall, Nicole's RDC, came in.

"All Midshipmen are ordered to report to the mess hall, where you will find your dates. Midshipmen Taylor, Robins, and Manning, I need to speak with you."

The others gave us a weird look and headed out, with a few see you's and a handful of have fun's.

"Midshipman Taylor, you and Midshipman Manning have been assigned to each other. The four recruit commanders will come into the hall last and will sit at the officer's table. Also, the four recruit commanders will start the dance."

I looked over at Nicole. "Do you know how to dance?" I asked.

"Of course, don't you?"

"London Proper?" I replied simply.

"Oh, just follow my lead."

"Midshipman Robins, you are to be Midshipman Jones' date."

"Isaac Jones? Sir?" Jade asked.

"Yes."

Jade took a deep breath, "Is it too late for sick call?"

"It's just an hour of eating and one dance. After that you can be free of the idiot."

"You think he's an idiot, too?" I asked.

"That's what the enlisted personnel say. I don't know about the Commandant, but…"

"I understand. I can do it. To the everlasting glory of the Fleet!"

"That would be getting him cashiered," Nicole said.

"I'll try," Jade smiled.

We slowly walked to the holochamber for the dance. For once, we weren't in a rush. I hadn't felt the freedom of having nothing to do since the last week at Dalton Spaceways. Thinking of Dalton Spaceways brought back some painful memories. I longed for the days with my old squad. I liked my new squad, but we hadn't fought together, rescued each other from death, or seen fellow squad members die. We weren't as close: we weren't yet family.

"Almek," Nicole said.

I jerked out of my reverie, and I saw that we were at the entrance to the holochamber.

"What's on your mind? You haven't said a word."

"I'm just thinking about my old squad," I answered honestly.

"Almek, you have a new squad," Jade said.

"Jade, it's been hard to part ways with my old squad. We had so much history, had done so much together …"

"Richard was inducted very quickly," Jade stated.

"Richard came in while we were still in a major jam. I almost killed him, and he tried to kill me. That made us instant best friends."

"So why aren't you a buddy of Jones?" Jade asked.

"Because Almek's an idiot," Jones said.

We all jumped. Jones was standing next to the holochamber doors.

"Commander," I nodded coolly.

"Midshipman," he nodded back.

"Jade," he said. "It's time for us to take our place inside."

Jade looked back at me as Jones took her hand. "Save me!" was written plainly across her face.

Once they had gone inside, Nicole and I went in. When we entered the room, we both froze. The hall, which just that morning had been a maze of corridors and small rooms, was now a spacious room, with tables scattered around the floor. At the front of the room, there was a dais with five tables of honor. The one in the center, reserved for the officers, was the largest, while the other four were reserved for the recruit commanders and their dates. Nicole and I went up to one of them and took our seats. Soon the two remaining recruit commanders came and took the other tables. When everyone was seated, the Captain stood.

"I could give a long speech about your remaining week, but I won't. I want to take just a couple minutes. I want to say how proud I am of each of you. We started with four hundred sailors. We now have three hundred fifty-two. By the end of the week, I expect we will be down to two hundred or less. So, have fun tonight, but get up tomorrow and prove me wrong. Let's see if we can end the week with three hundred. Now, dig in!"

I turned to Nicole. "Can you handle the heat?"

"I am the only female recruit commander, and I want to captain a spaceship. I will handle it if it kills me, or I'll join the Space Force."

"I've got a friend in the Force."

"Who?"

"One of my old squad mates, Kai. He's training to be an aviator."

"Cool. Aviators are definitely the best of the best."

"Yeah, that they are. Anyway," I said. "What's your history?"

"My dad's in the Fleet. Chief Petty Officer Taylor on board the SFS *Bravura*. It's a battleship, one of the finest in the Fleet. My mom's a snipe, an engineer. Ensign Taylor stationed on Luna Base."

"Ensign?"

"She's a mustang ensign, Almek. She transferred to the officer track last year."

"So you already outrank your father, and you hope to outrank your mom?"

"Yeah, my dad has to call me ma'am now."

We shared a laugh over that.

"So, just following family tradition?"

"Yeah, pretty much. I spent most of my life onboard the SFS *Robert E. Lee*, a top-of-the-line Fleet carrier. I first dreamed of flying Vipers, but my mom convinced me not to do that."

"Being an officer isn't easy," I commented. "And if you add on to that flight school…"

She just started laughing, "Almek, you're a born officer, why do you think being an officer is hard?"

"No," I said. "I may be a leader, but I'm not a born officer. I still view things by the rules of London Proper. Things are very different here."

"If you don't mind talking about it," Nicole began, "could you tell me about London Proper?"

So I did. I told her things about London that only Jenny and Annabeth knew. It was good to find someone to confide in.

The Captain stood up again. "Now for the dance. Everyone, attention!"

Everyone jumped out of their seats. Most of the tables disappeared, as the room was converted into a giant dance hall, with a couple tables left along the edges of the room.

"Now, for the real challenge," Nicole smiled.

She led me onto the dance floor, and a waltz came over the loudspeakers. Nicole took my hands; she placed one on her hip and the other in her hand. She then led me. I spent most of the time watching her feet. Until I picked up the beat, and then we danced with relative ease. Nicole started a line of questioning I hadn't expected.

"So, you like Jade," it wasn't even a question it was just a statement.

"Is it that obvious?"

"To Richard, maybe not, to Bronski definitely not, to Jade and me, yeah.

"Jade knows?" I was horrified.

"Don't get worried. She also understands what you're doing. You know that Jade is the best navigator in this batch of midshipmen, and you need her. You can't date her, because you want her to serve on your starship."

"Yeah, that's right, but does she like me?"

"Almek, knowing the answer will not make this easier. Remain professional, but ask her to dance at least once tonight."

"Is that an order, commander?"

"Don't give me that crap, Almek. I know that you are going to outrank me, before the war is over."

"Why do you say that? I'm lost in a sea of midshipmen."

"Don't make me laugh, Almek. Every officer and enlisted person here knows who you are."

"That doesn't mean much. Those officers won't continue on to the Academy."

"I seem to remember you met a fairly famous admiral at Dalton Spaceways, was it Andrus? No, that's right, you met the Sky Marshal."

"Nicole, I met him, I talked to him a couple times. It wasn't a big deal."

"He swore you in, you rode on his personal yacht. If that's not a big deal, I'm a Brit." A second later, she realized what she had said. "No offense intended."

I laughed. "Nicole, it's not a big deal."

Then the song ended, and a fast-paced swing dance came on.

Nicole sighed, "I was never a swing dancer. You're free to go now. Ask some other girl to dance."

"Okay, I call the last dance, though," I said.

"Okay, you've got it."

I wandered around the edges, and then a slow song came on. I spotted Jenny and flagged her down. I got there just as another midshipman walked up to her.

"Jen, how are you?"

"I'm doing great," she said. "Almek, meet Peter Armistead."

"Peter," I said putting my hand out to the midshipman on her arm.

"Please, all my friends call me Arm."

"Arm?"

"Yes, it started in elementary school as a gibe, but I grew to like it."

We headed out to the edge of the dance floor to find a table.

"So what's your story, Arm?" I asked him, once we sat down at a table.

"Well, my family's been in the MC for decades," Arm said. "My pa just about disowned me when I joined the fleet, but I want to fly, and the MC doesn't have any spacecraft. There isn't anything that can compare to a Viper. I want to be a Fleet aviator, even though the Marine Corps is in my blood."

"I've got a friend who's training to be an aviator in the Force."

"Yeah, Jenny told me about Kai. He seems like my type of person. I'd like to meet him."

"I'm sure you will." I could already feel the connection. Arm had just joined the squad.

We talked awhile longer, but once I heard a good slow song come up, I asked Arm if I could dance with Jenny.

"Of course," he said smiling. "No one will ever be able to control Jenny. She does whatever she wants."

Jenny just smiled at him, and I laughed. He was going to fit in great.

"I see you were paired with Nicole," Jenny said, once we had started to dance. "How was dinner?"

"Dinner was great. It was really nice to talk. She wants to be a captain. She says that I'll outrank her one day, but I bet she'll outrank me in the end. She would make a top-notch admiral."

"She could be your first captain when you're an XO."

"No, the Sky Marshal will put me with someone I don't know."

"Yeah, I guess that's true."

"Can you believe it, Jen," I said. "One more week, that's it, and then we're off to the Academy. A year ago, I would have laughed if you'd told me I would be here today."

"I would have too," Jenny said.

We didn't say anything else. We just danced together. It felt weird, but it was pleasant. Jenny was now the only member of my original officers' cadre still with me, and I valued every moment I had with her. When the song ended, she moaned. "Can we dance the next song, too?"

"Fine, one more song. I'm getting tired of dancing, though."

After that song, the next one was a fast song. Jenny turned to me, and she smiled. "You'll have one song to locate her, then the next slow song will be on. So, go dance with Jade!"

I didn't bother arguing. I went to find Jade, but instead I found Kris sitting at a table all alone, and I realized that I hadn't spent much time with her since we arrived at Boot Camp.

"What's up, Kris?"

"Nothing, much," she said.

"What happened to your date?"

"I'm not sure. After the dinner, he just disappeared."

"What have you been up to? You haven't been eating at my table."

"I've just been taking classes. And I haven't been eating at your table, because you're an officer."

"So," I said. "I don't care. You're a friend."

"I know that, Almek, but we aren't supposed to be friends. Officers aren't supposed to be buddies with enlisted personnel."

"Kris, will you start eating at my table?"

"Did I eat at your table in London Proper?"

"No, but we always talked."

"Yes, sir. I was your liaison with the soldiers, but I was not your friend."

"Well I guess you're right," I said, standing up.

"I'm always right, sir."

I smiled at her. "I'll see you in the sims then."

She nodded, and I went off in search of Jade again. I finally found Jade dancing, with a long line of male midshipmen waiting for the next song. I stood to the side pretending not to be watching, and when the song ended, I swooped in before the midshipman at the front of the line had a chance.

"Almek!" Jade said gratefully.

"Are you enjoying yourself?"

"No! I may hit the sack early. I seriously can't handle one more dance."

"Let's dance towards the wall, and we can sit down and have a drink."

"That sounds great!"

"So how was Jones?"

"You won't believe it, but he was a perfect gentleman. He actually seemed like a great guy. He seemed genuinely interested in me."

"It had nothing do to with your looks?" I asked skeptically.

"Almek," Jade said laughing. "You've noticed I'm a girl?"

"Jade, let's not go there."

"You started it."

We chatted until the song ended. Then Jade looked around frantically, "Let's sit down now!"

We made a beeline for a table, but before we got there, a tall midshipman who looked about nineteen stepped in front of me.

"May I have this dance?"

"Excuse me, I am escorting this midshipman to a table for a rest," I said.

"I think it should be the midshipman's decision," he said.

"She has already decided, so please excuse us."

The midshipman glanced down at my right chest pocket to read my name plate.

"Sorry, Midshipman Manning, I didn't realize that Midshipman Robins was with you."

"The error is forgiven Midshipman..." I read his name plate, "Palmer."

"Thank you, Midshipman Manning."

We made it to the table, and Jade stared at me.

"You already act like a captain," she said, amazed.

"I learned that from the Sky Marshal. He emanates authority. Anyway, it seemed to work this time."

I ordered a root beer, while Jade drank a coke. We drank in silence until Jones sat down next to Jade.

"Commander," I nodded.

"Midshipman," he nodded back and turned to Jade.

I felt an urge to reach out and snap his neck. Why was I letting an idiot like Jones date Jade?

*Because you don't want to date her,* Jenny said.

*Sorry, Jen.*

*I'm just trying to stop you from doing something stupid or closing the link.*

*Ending link.*

"Excuse me," I said, standing up.

"See you later, Almek," Jade said.

"Almek," Jones said.

"Yeah," I responded, turning back to face him.

"I'm sorry for calling you an idiot."

I was stunned. Was Jones just playing with me? Unsure of what to say, I turned around and stalked off. The dance was still scheduled to go on for another two hours, but I didn't feel like dancing anymore. I had danced with Nicole, Jenny, and Jade. That was good enough. So I looked for Nicole and asked her for one last dance before I headed off to hit the sack. Nicole and I talked about the Academy and our future careers. After that dance, I returned to my barracks, ready to return to the rigors of Boot Camp.

# Chapter 16
## Simulations

We made it halfway through the week before things got really rough. The classes we had been taking ended at that point, and we started running simulations. We did everything from damage control teams putting out fires to running flight simulations. These simulations were sometimes done with one hundred people and other times only five or six. I had been doing just fine in all of the simulations until we reached the fourth day. This particular simulation was to be run with just my friends.

We found our chamber and plugged in the memory orb Rogers had given us. I was to be the ACICO. Jade, of course, would be conning the ship. Richard was going in as Chief Engineer. Jenny was joining me in CIC. Bronski was a fighter pilot, as was Nicole Taylor.

I walked through the door and found myself in CIC. We had been assigned a medium-sized cruiser by the name of *Athena*. Though she wasn't much of a ship in raw size, she was armed to the teeth with the best and fastest weapons in the Fleet.

I saluted my department head, Commander Fredricks.

Great I have to deal with Fredricks again, I thought.

"You must be our new assistant CIC officer," he said. "Your post is over there." He pointed to a spot in between three enlisted men manning computers. "During combat, you will wear full combat attire and clip your self to the tie-downs at your post. You will learn what your enlisted are doing, so that hopefully you will be useful at some point."

I walked over and began talking with my enlisted.

One and a half hours later, the general-quarters klaxon went off, and I stood at my post, while the enlisted ran to the combat suit closet. Once my enlisted returned, I climbed into my suit. I looked over at Jenny, and we nodded to each other.

"CIC, report!" the captain barked over the circuit.

Commander Fredricks looked over at me. "Ensign."

I glanced down at the screens one last time. There were three ships closing fast. The computer said they were UME fast cruisers. I relayed that information to the commander, and he relayed it back up to the captain. Then one of my enlisted looked up at me.

"The bogey designated as alpha two appears to be dropping mines."

I nodded, "Captain, this is Ensign Manning, alpha two is dropping mines, I suggest we alter our course three degrees up and four to port."

"Ensign, that is Commander Fredricks' job. However, I agree."

The *Athena* moved slowly up and to port.

"I recommend we launch fighters to disable the mines," Jenny suggested.

"I disagree, but thanks." Fredricks replied.

Jenny nodded and turned back to her post. I could see the advantage of such a move, and I was willing to bet the captain could also, but …

"Alpha three is turning on us. They are within firing range!" a watchstander interjected.

"Alpha three is on a firing run," I shouted to the commander.

"Alpha three has launched missiles!" the same watchstander reported.

"Captain we have missiles inbound!" I shouted.

"Launch chaff! Jade get us moving faster. Bring us forty-five degrees to starboard and ten down!" the Captain ordered.

"Launch chaff!" I echoed.

"Ay, ay, launching chaff," one of my enlisted echoed.

"CIC, lock lasers on alpha three, fire missiles on alpha one and two," the Captain ordered.

"Lock lasers on alpha three, fire missiles on alpha one and two," Fredricks echoed.

The order was repeated by the appropriate enlisted.

"Lasers locked," I heard an enlisted shout.

"Captain, lasers are locked," I relayed.

"Fire, and keep firing!"

"Fire, aye, aye!"

The silence in CIC was eerie, as I knew we were firing round after round of laser volleys at the cruiser behind us.

"Their shields are holding!"

"Launch all fighters and bombers!" the captain ordered.

I saw the display in front of Petty Officer Brown, one of my enlisted, light up with friendly ships. The *Athena* had a decent squadron of fighters and bombers. She had ten fighters and five bombers. Those fifteen ships flew at alpha three. Then I saw something terrible appear on the screen.

A monarch class battleship had just exited k-space a light minute away.

"Captain, we have a monarch ahead of us at one light minute!" I shouted.

"Understood," the Captain said. "Robins, turn the ship around one-eighty. We'll blow up alpha three and collect our squadron. Then get us out of here at K-3!"

The squadron flew around alpha three and blasted her to pieces, and then we rocketed past, launching missiles and firing rounds of lasers into her hull. The last fighter landed in our docking bay, Jade punched the ship up to K-1, and nothing happened. We saw alpha three explode behind us, and the monarch was closing fast with alpha one and two. The Monarch had also launched a massive volley of fighters at us.

I heard the captain call for help on a tight beam back to Luna Base, but it was too late.

"This is Bronski commanding the squadron, I request new orders."

"Bronski," the captain said. "Engage the enemy fighters, and good luck! CIC you have permission to fire lasers at any fighter you can get a lock on."

I watched the screens light up with laser fire, but few of the fighters were destroyed.

"This is Bronski, I request rockeye backup!"

"I confirm that," I said. "The fighters are close enough that each rockeye could take out five of them."

"It could also take out our squad. Request denied," Fredricks said.

Anger erupted in me, and I reached for the automatic at my hip.

*ALMEK! It's a stupid simulation, and you're being watched by the RDCs and the officers. This is not the streets of London Proper!* Jenny screamed in my head, and shocked me out of my stupidity.

"Captain, I recommend countermanding that order, sir. We've lost two fighters already. They need better backup than just laser fire."

"Ensign, do I have to relieve you?"

"No, sir!"

"Sir," Petty Officer Brown said. "The monarch has increased speed to half-light. She will be within firing range in two minutes."

I relayed that information to Fredricks, and he passed it up to the captain.

"This may be the end," one of my enlisted said.

"Then we'll fight to the end. This is the *Athena*," I said.

"*Athena*, this is Lunar Base. We have launched ten fast cruisers. They will arrive in sixty seconds."

"Thirty seconds after the monarch," I told the captain.

"The *Sky* is behind them, but it will be another five minutes."

"We can't make it," the same man said again.

"Petty officer you are relieved. Senior chief!" I shouted, and he was at my elbow. "Can you run this station, senior chief?"

"Yes, sir," he replied.

"Then do so."

"The monarch is on top of us!" the senior chief shouted. "We're being riddled with missiles and lasers."

"Senior chief, launch all aft torpedoes at the brute," the captain said.

"Launching all aft torpedoes, sir," the senior chief echoed.

The torpedoes blasted through the shields and hit home. There were only five of them, but they worked wonders.

"Sir," Richard said over the all-hands circuit. "The Kelven drive is operational again."

"Sir," the senior chief said. "We just lost our last fighter."

I relayed the information to the Captain.

"Get us out of here, Lieutenant Robins," the Captain ordered.

We left the battle crippled, but alive. The volley of lasers and missiles had knocked out our shields, long-range sensors, most of our lasers, our gravity generator, and many other minor systems. We were later informed that the monarch retreated as soon as the *Sky* appeared. Bronski and Nicole had died not long after the captain had rejected the use of the rockeye missiles.

We continued the simulation for another couple hours, while nursing the ship through repairs. We came out, and we were met by Petty Officer Rogers.

"Almek," Rogers said, looking fierce. "I need to talk to you, now!"

*I told you,* Jenny said.

*Shut up,* I retorted.

"Almek, what were you playing at in the combat information center?"

"When?" I asked.

Rogers swore at me. "You know when, Midshipman."

I knew things weren't looking good, because Rogers had called me midshipman. He hadn't done that since the second day at Boot Camp.

"When I almost drew my weapon?"

"Yes," Rogers said, practically breathing fire with every word. "The Solar Fleet and the Space Force are the only two navies in the history of the world that allow even the most junior officers to carry handguns onboard. We allow handguns in case of a rapid boarding team, so we'll be prepared. However, you just supported the one argument as to why JOs shouldn't be allowed to carry weapons. If you hadn't displayed amazing ability earlier, you may have been sent home today after the stunt you pulled."

I couldn't believe what I was hearing.

"Mutiny is a serious offense," he repeated. "The Sky Marshal was pulled in to review this sim."

Oh, crap, was the only thing going through my mind. I really blew it this time.

"The Sky Marshal gave the Commandant very specific instructions that you were to be reprimanded severely, and if this ever happens again the Sky Marshal will come up here to talk to you personally. He would most likely dismiss you from the service with a dishonorable discharge and a down-check that would mark you forever."

I stood in silence for a while, trying to soak it all in. I was just one wrong move away from being a complete nobody. As a mutineer, I didn't think even the risk-taking Jack Dalton would allow me into the Space Force.

"Do you understand this, midshipman?"

I snapped to attention, and barked out, "Sir, yes, sir!"

"Good," he said, his expression not changing. "Dismissed!"

I dropped my salute, did an about-face, and marched away. As soon as I turned a corner, I put my back to the wall, and slowly sank to the floor. Before I could really start to dive deeply into sorrow, I felt a familiar voice.

*Almek, what's wrong,* it was Annabeth.

*I really messed up,* I told her, and then went on to describe the sim.

We talked for hours, discussing mutiny, officers, and the Fleet. Finally, she told me she had schoolwork to do.

*Ending link,* I replied.

*Good luck.*

It was at that point that I got up and, as I turned the next corner, I saw Nicole.

"Nicole," I said.

"Where have you been?" she asked. "You never showed up for dinner. You had the whole squad worried, and we are scouring the camp for you."

"It's a long story, and one I don't want to share right now."

"Okay," Nicole said. "Let's find the others."

We rounded up everyone, and I told them that I had needed some time alone. We then went to math tutoring with Richard. After everyone had gone to bed, I got a combined communique from Richard and Jenny.

*Opening link,* I replied formally.

*Why couldn't we get a hold of you?* Jenny asked. *We were really worried when we both got a reply saying that your implant was disconnected from the network.*

*I set up a program to avoid being interrupted,* I explained. *I was talking to Annabeth, and I needed to be left alone. I'm not ready to discuss it yet. I'm alive, so stop worrying. Ending link.*

I quickly ended the link, as I did not want to talk about this anymore. To my surprise, I didn't get another request for a link, and I drifted into dreams of London Proper.

# Chapter 17
## Battle Station Drill

The last day of Boot Camp was upon us. We still didn't know what we would be doing. We ate breakfast, anxiously waiting for the Commandant to stand up and tell us about the battle stations drill.

I glanced around the table, which had been gradually growing in size since the start of Boot Camp. I had put together a fairly large squad.

"Any guesses?" I asked, referring to what we would be doing for our final sim.

"It has to be a battle," one of the newer squad members, Stephanie Walker said. She was one of Arm's friends, and he had brought her into the squad.

"Yes," Armistead replied. "But what type of battle? Do you suppose we'll each run the same simulation?"

"The Kobayashi Maru," Richard said.

"The what?" I asked, raising an eyebrow at Richard.

"The Kobayashi Maru," he explained. "It comes from one of the old 2D TV shows. 'Star Trip,' or something like that, but Kobayashi Maru has become standard parlance for the no-win scenario."

"A no-win scenario?" Jenny said. "Almek wouldn't like that."

"Shut up," I said.

"Seriously," Nicole said, bringing us back to the simulation. "Will it be a Kobayashi Maru, or will it just be a massive battle?"

"Massive battle is my vote," Brad Palmer, one of Arm's friends, said.

"I say it'll be a Kobayashi Maru," Richard said.

"I just want to fly a Viper," Arm replied, as usual, only worrying about getting in a cockpit.

After what seemed like a decade, the Commandant finally stood. "Midshipmen and sailors," he began. "During the past week of sims, we have lost another fifty men. After today, we will probably lose another fifty. The Solar Fleet needs every one of you, but the Solar Fleet only wants competent sailors. So, be competent sailors. Everything will *not* go your way during this last sim. React appropriately, and you will go on to serve in the Fleet.

"This last simulation is an all-out battle against the UME. I will be acting the part of the Sky Marshal and each RDC and officer will have a corresponding place of command. Very few midshipmen will actually be in command during this simulation, but we will be scrutinizing how you handle your post.

"Report to your RDC to receive your assignments. Then report to the holochamber and board your new ship." The Commandant walked out of the mess hall, no doubt to allow himself enough time to get ready.

Before we could even stand up, Petty Officer Rogers was at our table.

"Petty Officer Rogers," I said.

"I have your assignments," he said, smiling.

"What are they?" I asked him.

He gave me my assignment sheet first.

ALMEK MANNING
BATTLE STATIONS DRILL
SFS VALIANT
CRUISER (SPACE)
CO - CPT. ALMEK MANNING

I glanced up at him, "Is this a joke, or do I actually get to command a cruiser?"

"Yes," he replied. "But, don't worry, it won't be a walk in the park."

"Why?" I asked him, a little nervous.

He handed me another sheet.

SFS VALIANT
CO - Cpt. Almek Manning
XO - Com. Isaac Jones
CICO - Lt. Com. Jennifer Kade
ACICO - Lt. Daniel Lee
Comm. Officer - Lt. Bradley Palmer
Nav - Lt. Jade Robins
CAG - Com. Peter Armistead
 Engineering Officer - Com. Richard Winters

"This *is* a joke," I said, looking up at him. "You've intentionally given me Jones for an XO and Lee for my ACICO?"

"I didn't, but the Commandant did, and I suspect he did so with orders from the Sky Marshal."

"The Sky Marshal does certainly seem to have an interest in your behavior and training," Jenny said, smiling at me.

*Thanks for the comfort and support,* I said. I read through the list again. "Where's Bronski, Walker, and Nicole?" I asked, naming the three members of my squad who weren't on the list.

"I'm an aviator under Arm," Walker said.

I noticed Bronski was still grinning at his order sheet and hadn't looked up from it.

"What's up?" I asked him.

Still smiling, he looked up from his orders, "I'm commanding a STAR team."

"As distinguished as the water navy's SEAL teams. Very cool," I said.

"It's always been my dream to join the STARs, but I didn't think I could make it."

"You scored superb on small arms," I said.

"True," he nodded.

"I'm the flotilla commander," Nicole said, looking at Rogers.

"Yes," he said. "And you're the only flotilla commander who is a midshipman. The other flotilla commanders are all ensigns. You'd better do well."

"Thanks," Nicole said. "No pressure."

"Congratulations, Commodore Taylor," I said, putting my hand out to shake hers.

"You didn't do too bad yourself," she said shaking my hand. "Captain Manning."

"Well," I said, standing up. "Shall we report to SFS *Valiant*?"

"Let's go," Jenny said.

"Remember," Rogers said. "The Sky Marshal will be judging this sim."

"As Nicole so eloquently put it, no pressure," I muttered.

I flipped over the page that listed my crew and read about the ship's stats on the way to the holochamber.

SFS VALIANT
Light Cruiser
K Grade (K-3)
Eight Laser Cannons
Two Torpedo Tubes
Two Anti-Fighter Turrets
Two Rocket Launchers

So the Valiant was a decent-sized ship. I looked forward to commanding her. I stepped onto the bridge, and I found Jones already sitting in his seat.

"X," I said. "I need to talk with you."

Jones stood up. "I expected as much, sir."

"In my stateroom." We walked through a side door and into my stateroom.

"What would you like to discuss?" Jones said, standing at attention.

"X, we haven't exactly seen eye to eye."

"Not at all, sir," Jones agreed.

"However, you are my executive officer, my right hand man. I need you to be on the same wavelength with me."

"Yes, sir," Jones said.

"Can we work together?" I asked.

"Yes, sir," he said. "Request permission to speak freely, sir."

I hesitated a little. "Granted."

"I hated the way you were singled out as being better than the rest of us. You were sworn in before us, you know the Sky Marshal, you seemed to be everyone's favorite, and I didn't like that. After we got into that brawl, I realized that your status wasn't as important as it had seemed at first, but you never gave me a chance to talk, and we never worked together in the sims. I am not your enemy, I swear."

I nodded. "I understand. What about Lieutenant Lee?"

"Lee," Jones grimaced. "I don't know why he hates you, but he does. It doesn't seem to be a logical hatred. He just *hates* you."

"Can I trust him to act as ACICO?"

"No," Jones said. "I honestly think he will try to screw things up for you."

"Thank you, XO," I said, standing up. "I'm glad to know we can work together."

"Same here," Jones nodded, and, with that, we walked onto the bridge together.

"We just received word from the *Sky,*" Palmer reported.

"What was the message, Lieutenant?" I asked him.

"We are about to begin drills. We are to stand by for orders and hold current position."

"Thank you, Palmer," I said. I sat down in the captain's chair. "Can you fly her, Jade?"

"What kind of question is that, sir?" she said, smiling at me.

We spent the next five minutes learning how to use the controls. Once we had reached ten minutes, we were starting to get confused. The time finally dragged out to fifteen minutes, then twenty.

"Did something go wrong?" Jones asked the question on everybody's mind.

The question remained unanswered as the time reached thirty minutes.

"This may be part of the drill," I finally said. "CIC, bridge?"

"Bridge, this is Kade."

"CIC, I want full spectrum scans going non-stop. I do not want to be caught off guard by anything."

"Yes, sir."

"Palmer, I want you to monitor all comm channels."

"Will do, Captain."

"Sir," Jade asked.

"Yes."

"Do I have the conn?"

"Yes. On the bridge this is Captain Manning. Lieutenant Robins has the conn."

"This is Lieutenant Robins. I have the conn."

"However, I do have the deck."

"Roger, you have the deck," Jade said.

Suddenly I was hit with a wave of memories. I could see my father standing on the Mayflower, "On the bridge, this is Captain Manning, Commander O'Brien has the conn." Even if it was just a simulation, I was a captain now, but what would happen under my first command…?

"Captain," Palmer shouted. "All frequencies are jammed!"

"XO, sound general quarters!"

Then the face of the Commandant appeared on all the view screens around the bridge.

"I am speaking to you as the Commandant of Boot Camp," he said. "I just received instructions from the Sky Marshal. He has requested this drill last longer than the customary handful of hours. The drill is now scheduled for five days. During that time, you will not leave the holochamber, unless your ship is destroyed. However, because of this change we will not be operating as a fleet, but just as a flotilla. Since each ship has only a skeleton crew, you will need more than your current skeleton crew to keep the ship going for five days. You will each receive new orders, and the holochamber will fade for five minutes. Find your new assignment and get ready."

The image faded. "The channels aren't being jammed," Palmer said. "I've got our new orders, sir."

"Yes, what are they?" I asked.

"We are all being transferred to the SFS *Nimitz*. That's the largest carrier in the fleet. We all retain the same jobs, replacing the RDCs and officers who were originally assigned to the *Nimitz*. The *Valiant* won't be part of the new flotilla."

The hologram faded, and we were back in the holochamber. We quickly rushed out of the chamber, and down the halls to the room where the *Nimitz* was located. We knew where to go, because that was where Nicole had been assigned as flotilla commander. We walked in, and the hologram was instantly back up and running. I walked onto the much larger bridge of the *Nimitz* and found Nicole sitting in the flotilla commander chair.

"Commodore Taylor," I said, saluting her.

"Welcome aboard, Captain," she nodded back at me.

"I'm going to call a meeting of all department heads," I advised. "Would you like to join us?"

"No," she said. "Just keep me informed."

"Will do."

\*\*\*

Half an hour later all of the department heads were gathered in one of the officers' wardrooms.

"Well," I said, leaning my elbows on the table. "We have a lot of changes to make here. First, X and Jenny, I need the two of you to set up watch rotations for the bridge and CIC. I want to have at least one person from the general quarters watch on each of the watch rotations."

"Will do, sir," Jenny said.

"Palmer," I said, turning to face my communications officer, who would serve double duty as supply officer. "I want you to contact Petty Officer Rogers, figure out how we are getting food, and then I need you to decide how to distribute it."

"Understood, sir."

"Also," I said, turning to Armistead. "I want at least five Vipers scrambled all the time."

"No problem," Armistead said.

"One last note," I said. "Jenny, I want you to put Lee on a CIC watch by himself and put a trustworthy enlisted, Kris Taggart would be good, on the same watch. When we are performing drills, I want to be advised of his performance. Also, please have the master-at-arms serve on the CIC general quarters watch team."

"Will do," Jones said.

"Good. Let's get 'er done."

\*\*\*

The first day was spent planning for the remaining days. That night was nice. It felt great to have my own room again. This wasn't something I had experienced in London Proper, but, at Dalton Spaceways, I had enjoyed it. The second day was spent on drills. We shot at floating targets and practiced fleet maneuvers. The aviators were allowed to show their stuff, doing precision synchronized routines in their Vipers. The third day passed much the same as the second day, but the fourth day did not.

I woke up to the sound of the general quarters klaxon. I quickly donned my uniform and rushed to the bridge. I checked my implant's clock and saw that this had happened at the absolute worst time for my ship. The midwatch had just been relieved by the morning watch. The reason this was so bad was that Jenny had just come off watch on the bridge, and Kris had just come off watch in CIC. This was bad planning on my part. I couldn't believe I hadn't caught this weakness in the rotation earlier, but now I faced a crisis when my two best CIC sailors would be tired.

I strode onto the bridge, and I saw that Jade was running things smoothly as the OOD. I took my seat and opened a link with Jenny.

*Jenny, do you need to hit the sack for ten or fifteen minutes? I'm sure that Lee can run CIC in the meantime.*

We both knew he couldn't, but that the enlisted could cover for him.

*I'm fine*, Jenny said. *On my way down from the bridge, I stopped by sickbay, picked up a pep up pill, then swung by the wardroom and grabbed my favorite coffee brew.*

*What would that be? And when did you start drinking coffee?*

*Three parts coffee, four parts sugar*, she said. *I started drinking this stuff about three days ago, sir.*

*What about Kris?* I asked.

*I did the same for Kris, and she told me she would be fine.*

*Okay, hold together down there.*

*Ending link.*

I looked up just in time to hear the boatswain's mate call out, "Attention on deck!" As Commodore Taylor walked in.

"What's the situation?" she asked.

Jade was the officer of the deck, and she answered. "We got an alert from Fleet COM. Two monarchs and various smaller escorts jumped at K speeds away from Mars orbit, and we didn't get a lock on their direction. All ships were put on full alert."

"Understood," she said. Then, turning to Palmer, as he hurriedly walked onto the bridge and took his spot at comm, "Palmer, get the Sky Marshal on the horn."

"Will do, ma'am."

"Arm," I called out over a separate comm channel.

"Armistead, here," he replied.

"Arm, I want all the Vipers and the B-101s ready for takeoff in five."

"Already on it, sir," Arm said.

"Good. This is it, so stay sharp."

"Aye, aye, sir."

I looked up again and saw the Sky Marshal's face appear on Taylor's display. Except it wasn't the Sky Marshal. I have to say it doesn't look right for anyone, but Sky Marshal Kitt to be wearing the single golden sunburst of the most powerful man in the Fleet. The sunburst just didn't look right on Captain Drake.

"We have five minutes before we will know if they're earthbound, or if they went farther out. If they don't arrive earth-side in five minutes, you need to be ready with welcome mats in about twenty."

"We will be," Nicole said. "Awaiting your update in five."

"Jade, I have the deck. You need to be at the conn."

Jade quickly moved over to the navigator's seat and relieved the JOOD. At that moment, Jones reached the bridge.

"You're late," I stated.

"Sorry, sir," he said. "I stopped by CIC and gave a quick pep talk."

"Good, idea." I said, with a smile.

"Thank you, sir," Jones said.

It seemed unbelievable at first, but over the past three days Jones and I had become friends. I knew that if I couldn't learn to love my executive officer, there was no chance the ship would run properly.

I quickly gave Jones a run-down of the situation. As soon as I finished, the Sky Marshal was back on with Nicole.

"They haven't down jumped yet," he said. "We are almost certain they are headed for you. Protect Ganymede at all costs."

"Understood," Nicole said.

Nicole started issuing orders to the fleet. Three minutes later, Jenny linked to my intercom channel.

"Sir," she said. "We just picked up two monarchs, three cruisers, and ten patrol boats. They're coming in hot. Recommend immediate attack."

I turned to Nicole. "What are your orders, commodore?"

"Use your Vipers and B-101s to take out the patrol boats."

"Thank you ma'am," I said. I quickly linked to Arm's comm channel. "Commander Armistead, launch all Vipers and bombers. Your orders are to take out the patrol boats. The *Nimitz* will provide backup for you with the big guns, once you weaken the PT boats."

"Understood, sir. We'll do the *Nimitz* proud."

"I know you will."

The Vipers and bombers launched, and I watched them collide with the enemy fighters. The British tornado is a good spacecraft, but it's not quite the equal of the Viper. I watched as the Vipers steadily took out tornadoes. Unfortunately, the tornadoes scored hits on about a fourth of the bombers before they reached the first patrol boat. The bombers dropped payloads of mark-five ion bombs on the first boat.

"This is bomb wing leader," a man said, opening a channel. "First target ready. We're heading out."

"Understood. Commander Kade, launch three torpedoes at the first target. Prepare the lasers to finish her off if needed."

"Will do," Jenny replied.

I heard the echo of my orders down the line, and then the torpedoes fired. I watched them shoot smoothly through space, and the first boat was down.

"Bomb wing leader," the man said again. "Second target ready."

We continued this process until we reached the fifth target, at which point the B-101s were forced to return and reload. The ground crew was ready for them and could load up a bomber in two minutes flat. The only problem was that we could only load five bombers at a time, and we had thirty bombers in our squadron. And most of the Vipers needed to be reloaded with missiles, since they had used up most of their searcher and talon missiles in the first few seconds of the battle. The Vipers were escorting the bombers in when they were hit by a fresh wave of tornadoes. The tornadoes must have been waiting in the hopes of intercepting them when they were low on ammunition.

"Captain," Jenny called out. "I've got thirty tornadoes approaching fast on the space wing. Recommend launching rockeyes."

I remembered an earlier simulation, in which we had not used rockeyes and had lost the entire space wing.

"Fire rockeyes in front of the approaching tornadoes. A scatter shot of four."

"Will do, fire rockeyes in front of the approaching tornadoes, using a scatter shot of four."

The standard thirty-second pause passed and the rockeyes hadn't fired. The tornadoes were getting closer to the space wing. If the rockeyes weren't fired soon, it would be too late.

"Jenny!" I shouted over the comm link. "Fire the rockeyes and report!"

No response.

"Palmer, are the comm systems working?"

"Yes, sir," he said.

I had one minute left before the tornadoes would be too close. I pulled up a panel in my own display and found the missile controls. I waited, as I ordered the rockeyes to be loaded, and then I fired. The rockeyes tore apart the first fifteen tornadoes, but the remaining tornadoes were too close to our own ships too allow another volley of rockeyes.

"This is Commander Kade," Jenny finally reported.

"What happened down there, Commander?" I asked.

"Lee, sir. He drew a gun on us. It didn't take long to subdue him, but too long to follow your orders. I am sorry, sir. I wasn't paying enough attention to him, sir."

"That's fine. Is the situation completely under control?"

"Yes, sir."

"Can we use our ship-based talon missiles?" I asked Jenny.

"No, sir," she said. "We're too close. The missiles would get confused, sir."

"Armistead, turn your Vipers around and engage the tornadoes."

"As you say, sir," he said grimly.

I watched the Vipers pull away from the bombers, all except for six of them that were deployed in a diamond around the bombers. I saw a volley of missiles from the Vipers hit the tornadoes, and six more went down, but not before they were able to fire on my Vipers. I lost seven Vipers in the first volley. Then my Vipers raked the tornadoes with laser fire. After the dogfight was over, I was down fifteen Vipers, but some of my bombers had reloaded. The ground crew had made enough room to reload one Viper at a time while cycling through the bombers. So, we soon had Armistead and five other Vipers fully loaded with talons and searchers and escorting the bombers to the sixth target.

I zoomed my display out to look at the bigger picture, and I saw that we were doing pretty well. The UME had lost more ships than we had, and the battle was beginning to lean in our favor, ... until I saw a group of three SF cruisers blow up, leaving a gap wide enough for another cruiser to fit through. Almost immediately, a UME cruiser fit right through that gap and aimed straight for Ganymede.

"Commodore!" I called out.

"I see it!"

"The *Nimitz* can get there in time!"

"But she has to take out the last two patrol ships."

"The Sky Marshal said…"

"Do it!" Taylor decided. "We have to stop it."

"Jade, bring us around."

"Bring us one hundred seventy degrees to port and fifteen degrees up," she ordered the helmsman.

The helmsman echoed her order. It seemed to take forever for the *Nimitz* to finish the maneuver, but finally she did. She sped up to intercept the cruiser.

"Commander Kade, prepare all weapons. I want to know the best possible moment to fire."

"Understood, Captain."

Finally we matched speeds with the enemy cruiser and opened fire. The firefight was vicious. Torpedoes streamed through space followed by volley after volley of lasers and grapeshot, used to weaken shields, followed up by missiles. We came out of the firefight in one piece, having left the cruiser badly damaged and hurtling towards Ganymede.

"Jenny, I need to know at what point the cruiser will collide with Ganymede."

"Calculating …," she said. "It will collide three miles from the nearest farm. We will certainly suffer civilian casualties."

"Commodore?" I asked.

"Jenny," Nicole said. "Can we knock out the cruiser before it collides?"

"Unlikely, with available equipment and time."

Nicole seemed racked by indecision. "Turn the *Nimitz* about," she ordered. "We have a battle to win."

The rest of the battle was uneventful by comparison. The *Nimitz* was badly damaged, but still functional, and with minimal casualties. We lost fifty percent of the space wing, but the hundred men lost in that wing had knocked out more than two hundred of the enemy. They had fought well. They would unquestionably be assets to the Fleet.

Nicole had just finished tallying up her losses when the simulation died, and we found ourselves back in the gray walls of the holochamber. I had almost forgotten that it was a sim. We were standing face-to-face with the real Sky Marshal and the Commandant.

"You all did very well," the Sky Marshal said. "However, Midshipman Taylor, the damaged cruiser launched escape pods filled with marines that landed on Ganymede and destroyed over half of our assets there, before the marines stationed on Ganymede were able to repel them."

Nicole's head fell in shame. "But," the Sky Marshal said. "You are only a midshipman and not yet a commodore. You did amazingly well in this scenario. You will receive the midshipman's cross for exceptional performance in simulation. Once again, good job."

"Sky Marshal," I finally said, deciding to ask what many of us had been wondering, "why did you change the simulation from one day to four?"

"Things had heated up with the UME for the past several days. I was really worried the war would start up again, and I would need all of you midshipmen to skip the Academy or just do a crash course. I wanted you to get a more realistic experience by extending the simulation."

"Have things cooled down?"

"A little, not much. It remains shaky, but that's nothing new. We may have a year, two at the most, before the war erupts again, but last week was the closest we've come to the brink under my command."

I realized that I could wait no longer to talk with the Sky Marshal about the Canids and the probability of obtaining better technology.

"Sir," I began, "request permission for a private conference. I believe there is a side effect of operation sixteen-twenty that has a direct bearing on current events."

The Sky Marshal looked intrigued. "Actually, I was already planning to have a private discussion with you to tie up one of the loose ends from this sim."

# Chapter 18
## Aboard the *Zochtil*

"Almek, as CO of the *Nimitz*, there is a matter of crew discipline that falls under your responsibility," the Sky Marshal said, once we were alone in his stateroom on the *Olympus*.

"Sir?"

"Midshipman Lee attempted mutiny under your command. Please give your recommendation regarding his performance in the sim."

"I don't understand, sir."

"There is the small matter of whether he graduates or gets cashiered. Please submit your recommendation."

I sensed that this discussion, and not the sim, had become my final exam.

"I need access to his personnel jacket to give a full assessment, sir." I continued. "Specifically, did he commit any other major infractions at Boot Camp?"

"None, except for a brawl he was involved in. Otherwise, his marks were excellent."

"That seems to settle the situation, sir," I said with some hesitation. "Midshipman Manning has about the same record, sir. I'd recommend they both be graduated."

"I'll decide what to do with Midshipman Manning, but I will carry out your recommendation for Midshipman Lee. Now," he continued, "what is it that I don't yet know about operation sixteen-twenty, in spite of the court martial?"

I proceeded to give him a quick explanation about the Canids, and their presence in our solar system. I also told him about the potential for a technology infusion.

\*\*\*

We disembarked from the SFS *Olympus* at Dalton Spaceways within three hours of completing the sim. The Sky Marshal's STAR guard was left standing on the quarterdeck of the *Olympus*. They were not happy about allowing the Sky Marshal to go into an unknown situation with only one partly-trained STAR midshipman to guard him. I looked over at Bronski. He was armed to the teeth with the latest in SF technology, and was lovingly holding a fully decked out special ops rifle in the ready position. He had taken to being a STAR well, and had been accepted into the STAR program, along with his whole squad of STARs from the simulation.

We had been instructed by flight control to dock our ship to the secondary ring of Dalton Spaceways. It was, in fact, not deserted, but was, as Richard had suspected, full of Dalton Space Force personnel. Soldiers and sailors were rushing back and forth, some carrying weapons that were a complete puzzle to the SF onlookers. Then I spotted Mr. Dalton, whose t-shirt read "Island One Colonist" and had a picture of the huge rotating space station colony on it. He had a small sidearm strapped to his leg.

"Welcome to Dalton Spaceways," he said as he approached us. "Sky Marshal," he said, nodding his head.

"Mister Dalton," the Sky Marshal said.

"Yup, that's me," Mr. Dalton said, smiling. "Okay everyone follow me, we'll be taking this trip in my yacht, the *Orion*."

"Will I be allowed in the control room?" the Sky Marshal asked.

"What the heck, why not? The Canids are decades ahead of me, so you'll forget about the *Orion* as soon as you step aboard the *Zochtil*."

" *Zochtil*?" the Sky Marshal asked, looking at me. "You didn't tell me about that."

Mr. Dalton turned to face me. "Haven't you briefed him?"

"I briefed him, sir, but we only had time for Alien Species 101. The Sky Marshal had so many questions, we never got around to discussing the *Zochtil*." I said.

"Ah," Mr. Dalton said. "And please don't sir me. I'm not in the Fleet."

"In fact," I continued, "about half of the people here don't have a clue why I'm making them waste their three-day leave here."

I turned to face the group, which included my entire squad. Everyone from Nicole and Jade to Stephanie Walker. "Those of you who have read the history books know that the *Mayflower* was engaged by an alien species, the Draconians. In fact, we were engaged by two species. One, the enemy, the Draconians. The other our friends, the Canids. Many have heard that the only reason we had any survivors from the *Mayflower* was a blue wormhole that picked up the escape pods and deposited them in earth orbit. That wormhole was produced by the Canids. The Canids have one ship here in our solar system, the *Zochtil*. We are going to the *Zochtil* to meet the Canids in person and make plans for how to defeat the Draconians."

I turned to face the Sky Marshal, who said, "What in the world are we waiting for! Let's go!"

Mr. Dalton led us down a corridor, and I was bombarded by more questions from the Sky Marshal. I answered them as best I could as we were walking toward the *Orion*. The ship was beautiful. I glanced at Jade, and I could see the longing in her eyes to conn this ship. Apparently, so did Mr. Dalton.

"Would you like to take her for a spin?" he asked Jade.

"Would I ever," she gasped.

We all took our seats on the bridge. Jade was directed to the conning station. After a tutorial from Mr. Dalton, Jade undocked the ship and took her out.

"What can she make?"

He smiled at that question. "K-7."

"What? The *Sky* can barely make K-4.5!" the Sky Marshal exclaimed.

Mr. Dalton just nodded.

After a couple minutes, Mr. Dalton took the controls again, and we were soon docking to empty space.

"Okay," he said. "We've docked and cloaked. Everybody out!"

"Sonnel!" I said, as we exited the airlock.

"Yes, Almek, it's me. Welcome aboard the *Zochtil*!"

"Sky Marshal Bartholomew Kitt," the Sky Marshal said, putting his hand out. "I represent the Solar Military."

"I know," Sonnel said. "I am surprised that Almek recommended bringing you so soon, but, after last week's scare, I sympathized with his position. I had originally intended to hide our presence from the command hierarchy of the Solar Military for another year or more, but it appears that Almek had other plans."

"I am sorry, Sonnel, but I do trust the Sky Marshal, and someone in the SF needs to know about everything. We urgently need better technology."

"Very true," she said. "Anyway, before we talk business and strategy, my XO, Ardent, will give you a tour of the ship. I will meet you in my stateroom in about an hour."

Just then, Ardent came around the corner.

Sonnel strode off, and Ardent took her place.

"It's good to see you again, Ardent," I said.

"And you, too, Almek. Welcome to the *Zochtil,* my friends. Though it may not be obvious, she was originally designed as a freighter and was only converted to a warship near the end of our war with the Draconians. Therefore, we are painfully aware that she is not up to spec as a Canid warship, but, unfortunately, she is all we have left."

He led us through the halls of the ship, and I spent most of my time watching Richard and the Sky Marshal. The looks on their faces were priceless. Finally, we went up onto the bridge.

"Attention on deck!" a Canid near the hatch said.

All hands got up and saluted. We all snapped to attention and returned the salute, except for Dalton, who only managed a perfunctory salute. Then Sonnel entered the bridge and led us to her stateroom. She waved us into seats that had obviously been designed for humans, while she sat down in a Canid seat.

"Okay, let's talk history," she said. Sonnel recounted her people's history, like she had previously done when we met her back on Dalton Spaceways.

"Why haven't the Draconians wiped us out yet?" I asked.

"The Garm," Sonnel explained. "After our home planet was destroyed, the Draconians were attacked by the Garm. The Garm are less powerful than the Zarc, but are endowed with unflinching tenacity. The Draconians and the Passerines are throwing everything they've got against the Garm."

"Then why wouldn't they just destroy our planet and colonies and leave?" Richard asked.

"They only have five rather weak ships stationed here."

"But we saw dozens!" I said. "What happened to their other ships?"

"They are holograms," Ardent said. "The Draconians stole our holo technology. They are simply material projections of ships. If the Solar Fleet threw it's most powerful ships at the Draconian guard, mixed with our superior scanners, you should be able to free yourselves of the Draconians."

The Sky Marshal looked like he was about to shout for joy.

Then Nicole spoke up. "You just fed us three centuries of history that included five alien races, I'm beyond lost at this point."

Ardent smiled. "I tried to explain that to the High Alpha, but she wouldn't listen."

"It's not that I didn't listen to my dutiful XO," she said to Ardent, before she looked at the rest of us. "It's just that I believe we can bring Almek's pack up to speed as quickly as we did Jack Dalton or Almek himself."

"Can't you download some history books into our 'plants?'" Richard asked.

"Yes, but that would be no more helpful than us having started earth history with The Rise and Fall of the Third Reich," Sonnel said. "We would surely figure out that Hitler was evil, but we wouldn't understand the context."

"Wait a minute," the Sky Marshal said. " Before we worry about what can be downloaded into an implant, I'd like to know when I can get access to the technology that's been issued to my men!"

"We can fix that," Ardent said.

"Slower," Sonnel said. "Now we're getting ahead of ourselves. Even with DSI manufacturing implants, they only have enough to keep pace with outfitting their own men. That is why we hadn't planned to contact the Solar Military for at least another year. We had wanted to get DSI up to speed first, so that together we could bring the SM up to speed."

"We've been over this before," Ardent said.

"Excuse me," Jade interjected. "Can I ask a question?"

"Yes," Sonnel said, raising a paw to silence the rest of us.

"Our goal is to defeat the Draconians. If we have the capability to do that, we need to turn our attention to the problem of the UME. We are on the verge of a system-wide war. If we can squash the UME first, we could then defeat the Draconians and move on to the stars."

"There's a complication you're overlooking," Ardent said. "It wouldn't be long before the Draconians focused more of their attention on you humans."

"High Alpha," a loudspeaker announced. "I'm detecting a ripple from the seventh dimension."

"The Passerines!" Ardent growled.

We all rushed to the bridge, and an image appeared on the main viewer of a towering humanoid figure with massive, blue-feathered wings sprouting from his shoulders.

"I figured you weren't dead, Sonnel," the Passerine said.

"No, I am not."

"I have reconsidered your father's argument, and, after stumbling into this blockade, I agree with him. We need an alliance. The Garm are pressing hard, but the Draconians are well positioned to win. If we can't figure something out, we will become their vassals or face extinction."

"I'm glad you've come to your senses, Numair."

"Our position has become desperate. Are you in a position to help us?"

"Working with you and the humans, I am certain we could defeat the Draconians."

The creature, the Passerine, looked at the Sky Marshal. "Is that a human? It looks like a Passerine criminal with its wings amputated."

The Sky Marshal laughed. "You look like an angel. Anyway, we need tech. We can't win without technology, especially since we face a multi-front war involving both the Draconians *and* other humans."

"You're fighting other humans?" the Passerine, Numair said.

"It's a long story," Sonnel said. "Will you commit your full support?"

"Yes, of course," Numair said. "That's why I sought you out."

"And you will not betray our existence to the Draconians?"

"Of course not. I may be stubborn, but I have not contracted Tilesian Dementia" he said.

"How can I believe you?" Sonnel asked.

"You will have to trust me. We will have to trust each other."

"I could still take you out," Sonnel threatened.

"That would be a brilliant way to attract the attention of the Draconian blockade."

"My forces are already mobilized," Mr. Dalton said, stepping forward. "You'll find five Independence-class cruisers closing on your position. I have faith that they can obliterate your ship."

The Passerine turned to read a display. "I've fought those ships before!"

"Yes, you have, and they won."

"So am I a prisoner?" he asked.

"Only if High Alpha Sonnel the Third of the Canid says you are," Mr. Dalton said. "I defer to her judgment in this matter."

I turned to the Sky Marshal. I saw that both his and Richard's mouths were hanging open and staring, not at the alien, but at Mr. Dalton.

"You have ships outside the solar system?" the Sky Marshal stammered, his usual poise having been toppled by Dalton's revelation.

"Yes, but let's not discuss that now," Mr. Dalton hissed.

Everyone turned to face Sonnel.

"I seem to have an advantage that I did not have the last time we met," she said. "Perhaps we should set up an exchange program to add some teeth to the laudable notion of trust. Since humans are so similar to you Passerines, I propose that you leave an ambassador here, and they send an ambassador with you."

"I'll volunteer," Richard said instantly.

"No," the Sky Marshal and I said in unison.

"I'll go," Mr. Dalton said, in a tone that admitted no further discussion.

"I'll leave my executive officer here," Numair said. "His name is Abram."

"It seems we have the beginnings of an alliance," the Sky Marshal said.

"Or, better yet, possibly the beginning of an interesting friendship," Sonnel said.

I nodded. "Maybe."

"I'll contact you shortly with the details of our exchange," Sonnel told the Passerine.

He nodded. "Excellent."

"End communication," Sonnel said.

I turned to Sonnel and wistfully observed, "While Dalton is serving as ambassador to the Passerines, I'm left moving on to the Academy and missing all the excitement."

"The war has lasted nearly a century," Sonnel said, "you may find that your time in the Academy passes by faster than you think. And I still trust that my reconnaissance mission in London Proper was not in vain."

###

If you would like to learn more about the author or the Almek Manning series please visit the author's webpage: http://www.almekmanning.com

www.ingramcontent.com/pod-product-compliance
Lightning Source LLC
Chambersburg PA
CBHW060811120626
46557CB00001B/169